THIRD DEGREE!

Carter grabbed Noreen by the shoulders, straightened her, and turned her until her nose was almost touching his chin.

"Look, lady, we don't play the game the same way, and your way is stupid. First you double-cross Maury. Then you go to the State Department, where you think you've got friends. Only you find out they don't send some idiot out here, they send me. Then you try to make like an amateur James Bond and you get your boy killed . . ."

He paused, out of breath.

"You through?" she asked, unruffled.

"Almost," he replied, dragging her across the room and seating her on the vanity stool. "Now, I want to know everything you know. . . ."

NICK CARTER IS IT!

FROM THE NICK CARTER
KILLMASTER SERIES

NICK CARTER

KILLMASTER

Blood Raid

CHARTER BOOKS, NEW YORK

BLOOD RAID

A Charter Book / published by arrangement with
The Condé Nast Publications, Inc.

PRINTING HISTORY
Charter edition / June 1987

ISBN: 0-441-57295-2

Charter Books are published by The Berkley Publishing Group,
200 Madison Avenue, New York, New York 10016.

PRINTED IN THE UNITED STATES OF AMERICA

ONE

Nick Carter stepped from the elevator to the rooftop of the Vendôme Hotel. Like everything else about the hotel, the rooftop lounge, pool, and dining area were luxurious.

Below the hotel, Manama, the gleaming capital of Bahrain, stretched to the sparkling calm waters of the Persian Gulf. It was difficult to imagine that, three hundred miles to the north, Iran and Iraq were blowing the hell out of each other.

The AXE agent lit a cigarette and let his eyes wander over the tables by the pool. The people all reeked of money. But why shouldn't they, whether native or tourist? If they were natives, they were all sharing in the country's oil and banking boom. If they were tourists, they were probably rich and here to hide their money.

He spotted her with a second sweep of his eyes. She was alone, at a table for two near the railing, away from the splashing children in the pool. The table and its neighbors were without umbrellas. She had probably chosen it for that reason. No one in his right mind would sit at such a table in the broiling midafternoon Middle Eastern sun.

1

The table provided privacy amid the nearby sea of humanity.

He pressed a bill on the passing waiter. "A double whiskey, neat. For that table."

"Yes, sir."

Carter moved directly around the pool, keeping her in his peripheral vision. The sun was hotter than hell, but Noreen Parris looked icy cool. In fact, her well-scrubbed features, devoid of make-up other than a little blush and lipstick, looked untouched by anything. Her long, naturally blond hair was swept back and held with a large clip, adding severity to an already severe face.

Carter knew better than to be fooled by the serene appearance. Noreen Parris was a vulture—a journalistic vulture. She had started her career on a scandal sheet in her native London. But that didn't last long. Since terrorism in the 1970s had been in vogue, Miss Parris had made terrorism her specialty. She was a bulldog when it came to getting a story, and she didn't care who she got her teeth into, or where.

Now she was a syndicated free-lancer with over a hundred European and American papers gobbling up every line she wrote.

As Carter approached the table he noted the clinging material and style of her lightweight dress. It did nice things to an already nice figure. The full globes of her breasts were center stage, and happy to be there.

"Miss Parris." It wasn't a question.

She looked up, studied boredom in her eyes. "Yes?"

"I'm Fields." He slid into the opposite chair and slowly removed the aviator-style dark glasses from his eyes.

"How do I know that?"

Carter sighed. "Yesterday afternoon you called Washington. You talked to a man named Harold McKnight in the State Department. You said you had valuable information that could solve assassinations and terrorist attacks in Europe, the Middle East, and the States."

"I also asked specifically for a high-ranking State Department official. You look like a spook."

The AXE man smiled but with no humor. "I am a spook. A very bad-ass spook. Your friend McKnight is a gofer. He kicked your call upstairs. Upstairs considered your info top priority, so they passed it on to my agency. That's their considered opinion, not mine, so I'm here."

"And exactly what is your agency?"

"None of your goddamned business," Carter replied, leaning back and lighting a fresh cigarette from the old butt.

"You're very blunt," she said, but managed a smile as she leaned forward to refill her coffee cup from a carafe on the table. In doing so, the scoop neck of her dress fell outward, affording Carter a splended, unobstructed view of her braless chest.

It appeared to be an accident, but he knew better. It wasn't. She tried to use it.

"Your eyes are bugging out, Mr. Fields."

"It's the sun. Did you know your right tit is bigger than your left one?"

She flushed and came instantly upright. "Now I know you're a spook."

"I'm also a male chauvinist pig, a mean son of a bitch, and I don't have time for bullshit."

"I gather you don't care for my profession."

"Oh, I admire your profession. I just don't like you and how you pursue it."

"The feeling is mutual. Shall we get down to business?"

"Fine." The waiter appeared with Carter's drink and scurried away. Her right eyebrow dipped when she saw the drink. "I'm a drunk, too." He smiled. "And always on duty."

She sipped her cold coffee and started in. "I've got an inside line on the killing of the Nigerian ambassador in New York, the bombing of the American embassy in Ankara, the kidnapping of the industrialist, Morton Weaver, in Caracas, the recent bombing of the Algerian legation in Madrid, and the killing of the Libyan chargé d'affaires in Rome last week."

Carter managed to keep his face a block of stone, but it was difficult. Handling the Rome meet with the Libyan, Ifeba Ghaffar, had been his baby and he had blown it.

The woman, the hotel railing, and the water behind her blurred in Carter's eyes as his mind conjured up the scene in the Piazza Venezia five days before.

He was sitting outside the little café, the roar of the traffic vibrating his brain. He was in the midst of seventy people, safe, not a familiar face among them. Not a single watchful eye like his own checking the crowd.

His gaze roamed the piazza for any sign of danger, anything out of the ordinary.

The traffic moved along quickly under the flailing arms of two back-to-back *carabinieri*, center stage on their little round cement pedestal. Behind them he saw a cabstand, the bored drivers paying attention to nothing. No pedestrians were loitering; they were all hurrying to or from their staggered lunch hour. Directly in front of the café, two black teen-agers vainly tried to kick life into an aging Vespa. The boy on the back, carrying a carpet roll, cursed the driver's ineffectiveness as he hopped from one foot to the other waiting to mount the scooter.

A normal day on the Piazza Venezia.

The stage was set for Carter to meet Ifeba Ghaffar. It had taken two full weeks to draw the man out into the open, at least ten phone calls to his contact at the American embassy.

Defect? No way. Ghaffar was loyal to his country, even if he didn't completely agree with its square-jawed leader.

No, Ghaffar wanted to assure the U.S. that the recent rash of bombings and assassinations was not to be blamed on Libya. He had proof that they were not. He also claimed to have proof naming the real perpetrators.

Invaluable stuff, if true.

Then he saw the little Fiat: red, white top, Italian license plate, no diplomatic designation, number 481—881. It stopped behind the taxi stand in a no-parking zone. The bodyguard/driver got out first. He looked around the piazza, and then across it to the café and spotted Carter.

The AXE agent nodded.

The driver went around to the passenger side. Ifeba Ghaffar got out. Like the driver, he was dressed in workman's clothes, a billed cap pulled low over his eyes. He hefted the briefcase from the car and started toward the café, dodging and weaving through the insane taffic like a native.

He was halfway across the piazza when Carter heard the roar of the Vespa.

The Killmaster looked. He saw the rider swing a leg over the machine behind his comrade. Half his right arm was inside the carpet.

The Killmaster knew, by experience and instinct, what was going to happen next.

He lurched from the table and crashed into a passing waiter. It was twenty feet across the sidewalk to the Vespa, but after ten of those feet Carter knew he would be too late.

The Vespa roared into the mainstream of traffic, heading into a direct line with the Libyan's crossing.

Carter watched, but could do nothing.

Suddenly the boy on the Vespa unfurled the carpet. Beneath it was a stubby Uzi submachine gun. The carpet had scarcely hit the pavement when the Uzi started barking.

The blast took Ghaffar full in the chest, fifteen slugs tearing a hole the size of his head through the middle of his body.

He sagged and fell, dropping the briefcase.

The rider dropped the Uzi, and in the same motion snatched the briefcase.

In seconds, the Vespa and its two riders were gone in the chaos that followed the killing.

"Mr. Fields . . . Mr. Fields . . ."

"Yes." Carter came back to earth.

"Are you always in the habit of daydreaming?"

He ignored her. "You say you know who hit Ifeba Ghaffar?"

"I said I had information about the assassination."

"Who did it?"

She hesitated, seemingly at a loss for words. The Killmaster didn't like it. Reporters were never at a loss for words.

He leaned forward, his face a hard mask, his voice low and as menacing as he could manage. "Look, lady, I was the guy meeting Ghaffar in Rome. I set it up, and he got blown away. Now, what have you got!"

Noreen Parris fidgeted and some of the icy coolness faded. "Actually, I've got very little."

"Well, dammit, give me what you have!"

She appeared not to have heard. "Are you familiar with, or have you ever heard of, a cult or group calling themselves the One Hundred Eyes?"

"Never."

"They are terrorists."

"Isn't everybody these days?" Carter growled in disgust, and signaled the waiter for another drink.

"This group is run by one man, a very powerful man."

"Who?"

"I . . . well, I don't know."

"Jesus," Carter hissed, "what the hell *do* you know?"

"I know that they are for hire . . . killings, bombings, kidnappings, you name it. You want your Uncle Louie snuffed, give 'em a call."

Carter got his nerves under control while the waiter dropped off his drink. He took his time lighting a cigarette and offered Noreen Parris the pack.

"I don't smoke."

"You don't smoke, you don't drink. Do you have any human vices? How about sex?"

"Occasionally."

"That's nice. Another question. Knowing your record, if you have all this information, why aren't you filing a story instead of calling us?"

It hit home. She leaned back and those icy blue eyes started floating around the pool, everywhere and anywhere but to Carter's steady gaze.

"Because I don't have the whole story, only bits and pieces. I need you to get it all."

"I'm listening."

"His name is Jabar Nanwandu. He's from Uganda."

"Terrific. Never heard of him. Who else?"

"I don't know."

"Lady, you don't know much at all."

"Nanwandu is frightened. He failed to execute a mission. Evidently, in this group, if you fail, you do it only once. About a week ago he contacted me."

"The expert on terrorism," Carter commented dryly.

"You must admit, Mr. Fields, I've written more on the subject than anyone else in the world. I think it's only natural that someone like Jabar Nanwandu would contact me if he wants to defect."

"*Defect?*" Carter barked, his voice louder than he

had intended. "What's this defect crap? Miss Parris, guys like this are scum. They may be bread and butter to you, but to me they're lower than a snake's belly. Assholes like this Nanwandu—if he is who you say he is—don't defect. They put their tails between their legs and run when the going gets rough."

She shrugged, but when she spoke again her tone was slightly less strident, more subdued. "Sorry, you're right. I couldn't think of a better word. He wants a half-million dollars."

Carter gritted his teeth and suppressed a low growl in his throat. He had gotten accustomed over the years to playing this game with the Russians. It had become almost a mutual understanding, a kind of gentlemen's agreement on both sides of the curtain: we woo yours, you woo ours.

But wooing a kill-for-pay terrorist whose fragmentation bombs kiled innocent bystanders indiscriminately wasn't his cup of tea.

He told her so.

"You can believe it or not, but I agree with you. But I also think that if this Hundred Eyes thing is real, and they are responsible for every instance that Nanwandu says they are . . ." She paused, shrugging again, knowing her point was made. As much as Carter hated to admit it, he knew she was right.

"You're prepared to pay him that much money?" he asked.

She nodded, the spine back in her body, some of the fire back in her eyes. "I haven't discussed it with my agent or any of my publishers, but I know I can raise that much on the story. Chances are, if it's accurate and juicy enough, I can get a book out of it."

"Yeah, I'm sure you can. Serial murderers and terrorists make good press."

For a brief instant, Carter looked down at his own hands and tried to remember all of his own kills. As the chief executioner for a supersecret agency like AXE, he had had his share.

But it wasn't the same. And, in his business, Carter didn't count the kill. If he ever did, he wouldn't kill again. Then someone else would have to do it, and perhaps that someone wouldn't be so precise and selective. Carter had the power he had—and the Killmaster designation—because he didn't make mistakes.

Noreen Parris saw the next question in his eyes and voiced the answer before he could speak. "It isn't just money he wants."

"A new identity, a passport, a hole to hide in?" Carter ventured.

"That's right. Things I can't arrange."

Carter leaned forward, close enough to let her expensive scent float around his face like an aromatic cloud. "Tell me something, Miss Parris. If all this bastard wanted was money, would you have called us at all? Or would we just read his revelations in tomorrow's papers?"

She opened her mouth to speak and Carter held his hand up, palm facing her.

"The truth!"

She rolled it around in her attractive head for a few seconds, closed her mouth, and studied the Persian Gulf.

"I thought so. Okay, lady, I think I can guarantee Washington will dance. Let's go get him."

"No."

" 'No'? What the hell do you mean, 'no'?"

"He insists on meeting you face to face first. He wants something in writing."

"Jesus . . ."

"He insists, and I think you'll agree he's in the driver's seat."

Carter leaned back in his chair, the disgust showing plainly on his face. He thought again of Rome and Ifeba

Ghaffar. Every hole had been plugged and every precaution taken on that, and Ghaffar had still wound up with a very large hole in him.

The Killmaster didn't like dealing with amateurs; they were too unpredictable. Noreen Parris was an amateur. And in this caper, he was not only dealing with her, he was in partnership with her.

It stank.

"When?"

"Tonight. You're staying here, at the Vendôme?"

"Yeah, suite five-oh-seven."

"I'll call when everything is set."

"Lady, I hope you know what the hell you're doing. If this Hundred Eyes outfit is as big as your boy says, you'll be lucky to keep him alive until tonight."

"He's safe, I assure you. I'm using a friend's villa. It's very isolated and defensible. Also, there is a bodyguard . . ." Here she paused, her stare as flinty as Carter's as she matched his glare. "He's a man like you."

TWO

Many miles south of the island nation of Bahrain, in Salala, the capital of the southern state of Dhofar in Oman, a tall, powerfully built black man glided down a dusty dirt street on the balls of his feet.

The street was narrow, bordered on both sides by a rabbit warren of tiny, whitewashed huts. The district was the Orianazi. It was the home for hundreds of foreign domestic and menial laborers who toiled in the capital. It sat in the stark, rugged hills three miles above Salala, and it was a maze to the black man's eyes. There were no addresses, only Islamic religious symbols on the doors.

The man's name was Adee Molnai. He carried a Cypriot passport that stated that his birthdate had been twenty-seven years before in Algeria. The years were truthful, but Molnai had actually been born in Uganda.

He had been in Oman for three weeks, and his work visa would be up in four more days. That meant nothing, because in twenty-four hours he would be out of the country.

He spotted the house he wanted and made directly for it.

Inside his destination, the man's female counterpart —a tall, statuesque black woman—stood in a tub of water vigorously scrubbing her gleaming ebony body.

She, too, carried a Cypriot passport, but not under her own name. Her true identity was Oranomi, and she was the wife of Adee Molnai. They had been married for one year, and in that time they had spent exactly one week together.

Yet both of them dismissed this inconvenience as a necessity. They were part of a great cause that made their personal need for each other petty by comparison.

There was a light tap on the rear door. Oranomi leaped from the tub and, still wet and still naked, rushed across the small room. Only when her hand was on the latch did her training make her pause.

"Yes . . . ?"

"It's me," came the whispered reply in the rumbling bass voice she knew so well.

She cracked the door and he slipped inside. It was scarcely closed and locked before they were in each other's arms.

"We must talk," Molnai groaned, his hands feverishly roaming over his wife's damp body.

"No. Soon, but not now," she replied, tearing at his clothes. "It has been too long, Adee. There is a bit of time now . . . for us."

Then he was naked and she was tugging him toward a corner, where a mattress had been thrown on the floor.

The man tried to protest, but he found that no words would come. She was on the mattress, tugging him down to join her. Suddenly he was in a time warp. There was nothing, no duty, no mission. He was in a void, drifting, aware only of her body and his desire.

Her body was supple, the curves perfect. Gently he kissed her belly, and his head swirled with the smell of her. It sharpened his hunger as he glided his hands over her full breasts.

She urged him on in their native tribal tongue. She was sinewy and resilient, entwining her arms and legs about him like a coiling snake. Her mouth was eager, catching his glistening tongue with a hunger greater than his own.

And then she was a dervish. Her hands swam over his taut belly, deftly stroking him. Her breathing was rapid, swelling and contracting her breasts.

His own breathing grew deeper as he lay on his back and she straddled him, swallowing him between her legs. Her warmth made his heart race and strive to match her eagerness.

Gently, he touched her breasts, fascinated by the flesh swirling in his big hands. He marveled at her taut stomach as her hips slid up and down, building to a rhythm that drove him to a peak of animal wildness.

He climaxed, but begged her not to stop. She didn't. She continued until she drove them both to a shuddering finale.

Minutes later, she rolled to his side. He studied her limp body in the semidarkness.

"You are full of such fury," he murmured.

"And were you a lamb, my warrior?"

They both laughed, and then it was over, the intimacy to be replaced by the real reason for his visit.

"The party is still on?"

Oranomi nodded and pulled a crudely drawn map from beneath the mattress. "The address is here. There is an alley in the rear for the trash to be picked up. The gate you will use is in the wall, here. I will unlock it at ten sharp."

"Guards?"

"Three marines, all armed. But they will all be in the front. You will be coming in through the rear garden."

Molnai studied the map in silence for several moments, then handed it back to her. "Burn it. Tell me about the guests."

She closed her eyes to concentrate. "Head of the legation, Sir Martin Ramsey. The two Americans, Albert Fischer and Jonas Wright. And there will be a representative of the sultan of Oman, but I don't know his name."

"Oranomi, don't tease me. The Russian . . . is the Russian still coming?"

She smiled. "Yes. They have been very secretive, of course, but I overheard a telephone conversation last night. Their security is so lax. They pay no attention to servants. They look right through us as if we were not there. The Russian is slipping across the border from Aden early this evening."

"The swine! He betrays his own people and uses our own traitor, Nanwandu, to barter for his defection!"

"What of Nanwandu after he found out about the Russian's defection?"

"Borassa has found him in Bahrain. After the Russian reneged in his payment, Nanwandu is trying to contact the British and the Americans. He is using a woman journalist as a go-between. Borassa and his people are watching her."

"Let us hope Borassa silences him before tonight."

"He will. Borassa has never failed!"

They sat in silence, staring at each other. Slowly, her hands came forward to excite him once more.

They made love again, slowly, with more tenderness.

It would be the last time they would ever touch. In eight hours both of them would be dead.

Carter flipped hot and cold about working with Noreen Parris as he rode the elevator down to the lobby. He was willing to bet the pension he would probably never live to collect that the woman would screw it up.

He had thought of following her from the hotel, but she had made it clear that she was going directly to her own hotel and not to the villa where Nanwandu and his bodyguard would soon be arriving.

The hell with it, he thought, moving to the overseas telephone exchange in the lobby. She was holding all the cards anyway . . . for now.

He gave the young woman at the desk the special Washington number that would be automatically scrambled from the other end, and took a seat to wait for the connection to come through.

He had been on the gig for over a month, and so far he had turned up only the Ghaffar lead in Rome. If this Nanwandu character was for real, it might be the break they needed.

The assassinations, bombings, and kidnappings that Noreen Parris had mentioned by the pool made up only a small number of the actual terrorist occurrences in the last six months for which no one had claimed credit. A large part of terror's success is based on publicity. When an act takes place and no group steps forward to claim responsibility, something is wrong, out of sync, not logical.

The CIA, MI6, the Mossad—and now Carter, representing AXE—had floated into the game.

David Hawk, the cigar-smoking, gruff-talking head of AXE, had been very specific in his briefing to Carter.

"It's got to be a private group, N3, with no allegiance to any country. We have word that even the Third World countries who condone terrorism are stymied."

For Carter, the logic was simple: murder for hire, terrorism for profit. He had seen it happen before, but not on such a grand scale.

"Mr. Carter?"

"Yes?"

"Your call to Washington is ready. Booth three."

"Thank you." He entered the booth and identified himself. Hawk himself was on the other end of the line.

The Killmaster talked for a solid five minutes without a break, bringing his chief up to date. When he finished,

Hawk's voice came back in an angry growl.

"The Parris woman is a British subject, but we might be able to apply some pressure through London."

"It would help," Carter replied.

"What's coming down soon?"

"She doesn't know . . . or she wouldn't say. She's playing it close to the vest, and I have a hunch this Nanwandu is doing the same."

"I don't like it, but for now it doesn't sound as though we can do much about it. I'll run Nanwandu through our computers. Hopefully, we'll come up with something. Agree to his terms, but make sure both of them understand that you control."

"Yes, sir."

"And, for God's sake, get a line on their next move. With any luck we can nip one before it happens. Also, we traced the Uzi that killed Ghaffar in Rome. It was part of a shipment made years ago to Uganda, when Idi Amin was still in power."

"According to Parris, Nanwandu was originally from Uganda. It's a starting point."

"Thin, but, yes, it's something. Stay in touch, Nick."

"Yes, sir."

Carter hung up and rode the elevator to his floor. Gathering dusk had given way to light from silk-shaded lamps along the paneled hallway.

Carter opened the door, and stopped cold two steps over the threshold. The overhead light was on and most of his clothes were strewn about the bedroom. The sitting room was an equal mess, with overturned furniture and the cushions pulled from sofas and chairs.

He stood stock-still, every nerve tense, listening to see if the intruder were still around. The bedroom, the half-open closet door, all fell under his line of vision.

Suddenly the phone began to ring. Carter resisted it for a moment, but the pull was too strong. He eased the door closed behind him and moved across the room.

He was halfway there when a bulky figure in a rumpled white suit filled the bedroom doorway. Hanging slack from his left hand was Carter's Luger, obviously discovered in the false bottom of his suitcase. Holding steady in his right hand was a standard-issue Webley .45 automatic, leveled directly at Carter's gut.

"Don't answer it, Carter. She'll call back."

Carter brought his eyes up slowly from the Webley to the man's sour, gray-bearded face.

"Maury Richland. I thought you had finally crawled into a bottle and drowned."

Maurice Allistair Richland was only around fifty, but he looked every minute of sixty-five. There were few whole blood vessels left in his florid face, and his nose was swollen and nearly as red as his faded eyes. The puffy cheeks beneath the gray beard were full of yesterday's excess, and it looked as though he had been sleeping in the suit for a week.

Richland had started out with MI6 as a low-level courier. He had progressed to being a low-level operative on the German desk, and managed along the way to hide his excessive drinking.

About four years ago he had blown his job, his pension, and two agents coming out of East Berlin. Carter had been in on that one, and looking at Maury Richland now, he was sorry he had kept his temper in check that night and not put a few well-placed holes in the man.

The two agents—one American and one British—had been killed. Richland had been cashiered, and disappeared.

"Where have you been keeping yourself, Maury, besides a pub?"

"You always were a bit of a smartass, Carter. Africa, mostly. You learn a lot down there."

"I'll bet," Carter growled. "Do you trust me to reach for a cigarette?"

"Sure." He moved as if he had never trusted anyone in his life. And even though his watery eyes had trouble focusing, he was all business. The arm with the .45 was stiff, but not stiff enough to freeze. He padded around Carter to the door like a wary tomcat and locked it.

All this time the phone had continued to ring. Suddenly it stopped.

"You probably made me miss a very important call."

"Like I said, she'll call back."

Carter tensed. *She? Noreen Parris?* Suddenly the Killmaster knew that the cashiered MI6 man had not paid him a visit on a whim.

"Sit, lad, we have to talk."

Carter lit the cigarette rocking between his lips and eased his powerful frame into one of the chairs.

"You got a bottle in that top drawer there," Richard gestured. "I could use a drink."

Carter shrugged. "Get it yourself."

Richland pocketed the Luger, shifted the Webley to his left hand, and moved to the desk. He fished out the bottle and took a deep drink, tilting it to his mouth like a nursing baby. When it came down he held it out to Carter.

"No, thanks, I'm working. Of course, that never stopped you."

Richland glared, figured it wasn't worth it, and drank again. The booze seemed to steady him a little, but he was still a mess.

Carter cased him further as the man let the liquor revitalize his body. Richland had looked like hell years before, but he had gone downhill since then. His hair was thin and dry, a tattered veil over a gray scalp. The face was beginning to fall away around a nose probably made pug in some forgotten battle of his blustering youth. The bulldog head appeared to be set on the shoulders without benefit of neck, and a belly protruded

mournfully from a too-tight shirt. Perversely, the
threatening pink-blue eyes contained the dying glimmer
of some choirboy supplication. He was full of fear, and
therefore dangerous.

He caught Carter looking. "I look like shit, don't I."

"Yeah, Maury. You look like shit."

The man smiled, but it was more like a leer. "But I'm
still sharp enough to connect. I lost that Parris bitch,
but I spotted you at the airport. It was just a guess, but
it worked. You led me back to her."

"Bully for you," Carter said flatly. "What do you
want from me?"

"Back in," Richland replied, the gun sinking out of
business range as he became more interested in the bottle.

Carter could have taken him then, but he suddenly
realized that he could learn more by coddling.

"Back in on what, Maury?"

"I didn't figure the bitch would mention me. How
much did she tell you?"

"Suppose you tell me first, Maury. Right now I think
I'm still in the dark."

Suddenly all the threat went out of the other man. He
flopped into a chair opposite Carter, the gun in his lap,
and started to whine. "Let's you and me talk business."

"I'm all for good, honest, free enterprise," Carter
said with a shrug.

"I found him."

"Found who?"

"Jabar Nanwandu. I found him and turned him when
he blew the Ridalli kill in South Africa."

Carter's mind clicked. It was about six weeks ago.
Ridalli was a priest. He had been sent to South Africa
directly from the Vatican as part of a negotiating team
to try and put whites and blacks together. Both sides
had sighed in relief when the bomb that had been placed

in his limousine went off prematurely. If the bomb had
gotten him, it very well could have set off new and even
more devastating riots.

"Go on," Carter said noncommittally.

"When he blew it, Nanwandu was scared shitless. He
couldn't go home again. By home, I mean this bunch of
crazies he works for. With them, if you fail, you'd better bite the pill."

"Who are the crazies, Maury?"

"I'll get to that," he said, and took another stiff one
from the bottle. "Anyway, I get to him. I tell him I can
put him up with MI6 and save his ass if he tells all."

"But he wanted money up front that you didn't
have."

"Right. By the time I find the bank account, the
stupid bastard has contacted some Russian."

"Who?" Carter asked.

"I don't know, but the Russian screwed him. Got his
whole story on tape and takes off. No money, no im-
munity. But I figure I'm in again. I put Nanwandu and
Noreen Parris together in Cyprus."

"Parris can come up with the dough, but you
couldn't come up with papers and a new life and identity for Nanwandu."

Richland gave the Killmaster a sticky smile. "The
bitch told you a little something, didn't she."

"A little," Carter said, nodding. "Go on."

"They split . . . Nanwandu, Parris, and her stud, a
guy named Collis. He used to work as a private bodyguard in London for visiting VIPs."

"What do you want out of this, Maury?"

"My pension back. I figure, if I bring this slime in
and he talks, London will have to reinstate me."

Carter doubted it. And he had enough on his hands
with Noreen Parris. But Maury Richland could make
waves, and for the next few hours, Carter couldn't afford waves.

"How much do you know, Maury? How much did Nanwandu tell you?"

Now the smile was sly. He tipped the bottle and left only about three fingers in the bottom before he spoke again. "I'm betting he told me a hell of a lot more than he told the Parris bitch. I'm serious, Carter—there's enough in this guy for all of us. At worst, I get a couple of years of good booze and women. At best, old age insurance."

"You still haven't answered my question. How much did Nanwandu tell you?"

"Get me back with him first, then we'll talk." He clenched the bottle and suddenly looked away.

Carter stood and made a show of pacing. In fact he was thinking, thinking hard. It was obvious that Richland knew more than Noreen Parris. If Carter didn't soothe him, Richland might be able to foul up the works by going to Nanwandu's employers before Carter could tighten it down.

He wouldn't put it past Maury Richland to deal with anybody.

Carter made a decision.

"I'll do what I can with London, Maury, but I think you know that's next to impossible. In any event, if you keep a lid on this, I'll get you a cash allocation from Washington."

The watery eyes flashed with interest. "How much?"

"If Nanwandu is gold . . . fifty thousand."

Richland went into deep thought. Carter tensed, waiting for an answer. He could terminate Maury Richland to keep him on ice. but he didn't think he would have to. And he didn't want to, especially if the whole Nanwandu business turned out to be a pipe dream.

And if Richland agreed, Carter was fairly sure he would stick with it. It was obvious that he needed somebody—anybody. He was shaking himself up to the finish line fast, with only a desperate dream to hang on to.

His days as a solo operator had drowned in the bottle he held so desperately in his hand. That's why MI6 had fired him. Carter needed him around for future reference, but in the meantime he must be kept in the deepfreeze. Or in alcohol.

"Well?" Carter said after a minute.

"I'm thinking."

In the meantime, the phone started ringing again, and Carter got up to answer it. Richland didn't object; he emptied the bottle and then studied it with great concentration.

"Carter here."

"This is Noreen Parris. They are here. Do you have a pencil?"

"Yeah, shoot." He didn't need a pencil. He memorized the directions and the address of the villa as she spoke them.

"I'm leaving in fifteen minutes," she said. "We should arrive at the same time."

"I'll be there," Carter replied. He hung up and turned to Richland. "That was Parris."

"I figured. Take me along."

"No way. At this point you'll muddy the waters. Have you made a decision?"

"A hundred thousand. Jesus, I *need* that much."

"Seventy-five. Washington will never dance for a hundred, even with Parris footing the tariff on Nanwandu."

Richland looked at Carter for a long moment and then seemed satisfied. Carter figured that even in his best days Richland had been nothing more than an office worker. MI6 wouldn't have let him loose in the field on anything more important than an inquiry at the information booth of Victoria Station. At the moment booze was helping him dream up a rosy world, with Carter propping him up along the way.

"Okay, Yank, you got a deal. But remember something . . ."

"Yeah?"

"I got a hate on, Carter, for the world. I got no tears for anybody . . . that scum Nanwandu, the Parris bitch, or you. Don't move out on me."

"You're a prince, Richland."

Carter got a second bottle, a pint, from the drawer and passed it to him in return for the Luger.

"Stay put. Be my guest," he said. "Order dinner from room service and anything liquid if you run out. I'll be back."

Richland was sprawled on the bed nursing the second bottle as Carter let himself out of the suite, locking the door behind him.

THREE

The haunting chant of the *meuzzin* had just ended the evening call to prayer as Lady Sylvia Ramsey stepped from her bath and lightly patted her body with a towel. It didn't take much. The stifling heat quickly evaporated the water. She powdered her body and stepped into the bedroom still nude.

"My dear, you're shocking!" Sir Martin said to her reflection in the mirror behind him.

"Aren't I though?" she said with a smile. "Here, darling, let me do that."

She moved around to his front and began adjusting his tie. As she did, he placed his arms around her and ran his hands down over her buttocks.

"Hear now, you cheeky boy," she chided, "we haven't time for that!"

His gray eyes twinkled. "As the head of the British legation in Salala, Oman, the foremost petroleum expert outside England, and as your husband, my dear, I have the right to cheek."

"Of course you do, but we still don't have time." She was taking far too long with the tie. "Darling . . ."

"Yes?"

"Don't you think you can tell me who our mystery guest is tonight? I mean, they are all arriving within the hour."

He looked sternly into her eyes. "Are you sure you're not a spy?"

"Not to my knowledge," she replied with a little laugh.

"Very well, then, I suppose you do have a right to know at this late hour. His name is Hadj Bal-Sakiet."

Her brow furrowed. "Never heard of him."

It was Sir Martin's turn to chuckle. "You wouldn't have, my dear. He is a very secretive man, keeps an extremely low profile." He looked at his watch. "I'd say that about now he's over the border from Aden and climbing into my car on the Oman side."

Alarm entered his wife's eyes. "Aden! He's a Communist!"

"Quite so. He was originally a marsh Arab from Iraq. He studied in Moscow and finished quite high in all his classes. So high, as a matter of fact, that he was granted citizenship."

This was a subject Lady Ramsey didn't feel like discussing stark naked. She pulled a light blue cotton robe over her body and sat at a nearby vanity to apply her makeup while the discussion continued.

"If he's become Russian, what's he doing here, in Aden?"

"He just happens to be in Aden in order to be close to Oman. Actually, he's quite a specialist in Arab-African affairs . . . rides with the Bedouin, breaks bread with the Pashtin and the Tajik, all that sort of thing. Actually, he's a major in the KGB."

Lady Sylvia whirled on her stool. "And he's coming to our dinner party?"

"Quite so, darling. He wants to defect."

"Oh, my God."

"What's the matter?"

"I thought they did that sort of think in Berlin or Vienna . . ."

"They do," Sir Martin said with a nod. "But, you see, this is a special case. He wants sanctuary in Oman. That's why the sultan's representative was invited tonight."

"That means you've been planning this for some time," she said, her eyes narrowing to slits.

"Actually, yes, darling. We just needed proof from this KGB bugger Bal-Sakiet that he had something worth trading for safe exile."

"And you got that something?"

"Bits and pieces, really, nothing very substantial. The man's quite cagey, you see. That's why we insisted on this little dinner party. He will give us a little more, and if we think it's good enough, he stays."

Lady Sylvia whirled back to the mirror and attacked her face again. "Well, for my peace of mind, Martin, please let this be the last time in our house. I hate Russians."

"Actually, my dear, he's an Arab."

"That's all right," she replied coolly. "I hate them, too."

At this, Sir Martin roared with laughter and shrugged into his dinner jacket. "Hurry along, darling, you haven't much time. I'll meet you below."

The tall, striking black woman, Oranomi, remained in the hall linen closet that adjoined the Ramsey bedroom until Sir Martin's footsteps faded down the stairs.

When she emerged, she had towels piled high in her arms and a broad smile on her face.

She had heard quite enough to ensure that Bal-Sakiet had not yet revealed enough to harm their order or their supreme leader.

As Oranomi walked down the hall, Lady Sylvia slid a green silk dress down over her hips. She checked herself in the mirror and, other than the concentrated frown on her beautiful face, approved.

A Russian-Arab-KGB major-defector at her dinner party? It was obscene!

It was also frightening. God only knew what the man might do.

Gently, she slid open the top drawer of her vanity. Her eye immediately found the small pearl-handled revolver that her husband had given her years before and taught her how to use.

Can't be too careful in these countries, darling. And you know what they are doing to embassies and legations these days. Best to be prepared.

Sylvia Ramsey never dreamed that, in less than three hours, that tiny, chrome-plated gun would cause her own death.

A cooling breeze from the gulf stroked and cooled Carter's face as he waited for the rental Audi in front of the hotel.

When it came, he tipped the driver and headed for the coast road. A half mile down the Bahrain coast, he turned inland and began to climb.

A fat red moon was just rising over the gulf, and there was the strong scent in the air of frankincense trees that grew wild along the roadside.

Eventually, the newer concrete highway gave way to a gravel, then a dirt road that twisted around hills and gorges, past new, modern villas and flowering hillsides.

Twenty minutes after leaving the hotel, Carter found the villa he sought, and slowed. It was partially surrounded by a high wall of pink stone crawling with bougainvillaea. Behind the wall he saw the tiled roof of a small, unimposing villa.

The gate was open. He turned in and found himself in a tiny, circular courtyard. A Mercedes sedan was parked near the door, a sticker with the name of a local rental agency discreetly placed on the rear bumper.

The car, he was sure, was driven by Noreen Parris. Even a rental, for her, would have to be a Mercedes.

The Killmaster cut the engine and stepped from the car to the flagstones. He paused.

It was too quiet. Where was the bodyguard?

As he walked to the door, the full fragrance of the flowers that nearly covered the villa's walls filled his nostrils like heavy musk. A slit of light was visible between the drawn curtains of a window to the right of the main entrance, but otherwise the house was in darkness.

Then he saw it. The door was open about a foot.

Carter drew the Luger, jacked a shell into the chamber, and flipped off the safety. He stood to one side of the door and very gently pushed it open.

Nothing . No sound, no movement, no light.

Cautiously, he fell into a crouch and darted into a short hall decorated with dark, parquet floors, a French provincial table, and a single chair. On the table was an unlit wrought-iron lantern.

Slowly, his Luger making an arc in front of him, the Killmaster moved down the hall to a small living room. There were a few pieces of expensive furniture against white walls, bare except for a couple of fading tapestries, a corner fireplace, a chaste, modern couch, and a large window with a moon-drenched view of the Persian Gulf in the distance.

And then he saw her. She was on a low stool near the far wall, almost hidden by the corner of the couch. She was sitting with her skirt hiked up high on her thighs, her arms hugged tightly between her knees.

"Miss Parris . . . ?"

No answer, not even a look. Still cautious, Carter moved into a crouch in front of her.

Then he saw her eyes. There was no fear, no shock. There was nothing. They were vacant.

He shook her shoulder. "Noreen, what the hell is it?"

She started to drop her head into her lap and moaned, "My fault."

"Dammit, what's your fault?" Carter rasped, although he felt a sudden chill run up his spine, as if he already knew. He lifted her head and at the same time stuck his face directly into hers. "Talk to me!"

"In there . . ."

"Where?"

A feeble hand came up, pointing. "Bedroom."

Carter stood and moved across the room, fast. She made no move to follow. She simply sat there as if carved from stone as Carter pushed the bedroom door open and stepped inside.

He was naked, lying on his back on the bloody bed. One look and Carter could see that it was a ritualistic killing. His genitals had been removed and stuffed in his mouth. The killing itself had been from a wire garrote. It was still around his throat, embedded a good two inches in the flesh.

Carter moved closer. The face was splotched purple where the constrictions of skin over bone had prevented the movement of blood to the body's lowest point. Death had given him two black eyes and bloody ears; the cigarette burns on his hands and face were extra.

Carter gently kneaded the livid area under one eye. Within an hour of death the blood could be pressed away. It had already fixed.

Carter slid a hand up to the armpit and felt the temperature. It was warm, but cooling fast. With difficulty, he straightened the bent left leg. Upon death, the human body begins losing heat immediately at a broadly predictable rate. The skeletal muscles begin to stiffen about four hours later. Rigor mortis is at its peak from twelve to sixteen hours after death, depending on the temperature of the immediate environment. Soon after, the enzymatic destruction of tissue begins, turning a body, after a day or two, as floppy as a rag doll.

Carter guessed he had been dead a little over two hours.

Turning his face to take a clean breath, he noticed the clothes on the floor. He went through them and found nothing.

He made a beeline back into the other room toward the woman, who still sat trancelike in the chair. He clutched her shoulders and yanked her to her feet.

"Which one is he . . . the bodyguard or Nanwandu?"

"Nanwandu," she choked.

"Shit," Carter hissed, and headed toward the rear of the villa for a look-see.

The sultan's representative was Sheik Musalam Al-Sir, a distant cousin of Oman's ruler, and, like him, conservatively progressive. He was tall, with dark, rugged features, his upper lip covered by the ever-present mustache. His dress was traditional, a dark robe over a full-length white *dish-dasha* cinched by a gleaming silver dagger, or *khanjar*.

His face was impassive as he stood, his hands clasped behind his back, listening to the two men from the American State Department and the Britisher, Sir Martin Ramsey, obliquely discuss the man who would soon arrive at the legation.

Now and then his eyes would stray to Lady Sylvia, who stood near her husband's side. It always amazed Al-Sir how these men could talk of such weighty affairs in the presence of their women. But he supposed that was the Western way.

His country, Oman, had been called "the Western world's jugular vein" and "the Gibraltar of the East." There were few places in the world that were so strategic yet so thinly defended. The twenty-thousand-man military force, trained and led by British officers, was one of the best in the world. It was also one of the smallest.

That was why Musalam Al-Sir had not yet agreed to

let the defector, Bal-Sakiet, remain in his country. The Russian KGB were famous for their double agents. This man could be merely a plant. Once established in Oman, and with a smuggled radio, he could do irreparable harm in a very short time.

Even now, a Russian Kresta II-class cruiser had anchored outside Oman's territorial waters. They were not there to watch the flaming sunsets. They were there to collate the 750,000 barrels of oil an hour that passed through the Strait of Hormuz, and to eavesdrop as much as they could on what went on inside the tiny country.

A Russian inside Oman with even a small transmitter could greatly enhance their accumulation of intelligence.

Yes, Al-Sir thought, whatever this Arab/Russian spy was bringing with him concerning a bloody terrorist cult would have to be very valuable indeed for the Omani government to allow him to stay in the country.

Al-Sir watched a woman in green move away from the group toward a sideboard. It had been the third such move in the last hour. Just as she had the other two times, she set down her glass of Perrier and slid her hand into a sequined clutch purse on the sideboard.

The routine was the same. She extracted a small silver flask from the purse, glanced around at the men to make sure no one saw, and brought the flask quickly to her lips.

Out of courtesy to the Moslem faith, Sir Martin Ramsey never served spirits at his dinner parties. That made it very difficult for his wife, a closet alcoholic, to make it through an entire evening.

Al-Sir had seen her resort to this subterfuge many times in the past. Normally, he really wouldn't mind. But this evening of all others, with the importance of their visitor, her drinking made him uneasy.

A servant appeared at the door. Lady Sylvia, on legs not too stable, tottered toward him. She bent slightly from the waist so the servant could whisper in her ear.

Al-Sir noticed that she was swaying, and when she turned to speak, her eyes had become very vague and glassy.

"Gentlemen, our guest has arrived."

Al-Sir's expressionless face masked his inner feelings, but he could not silence a nagging concern in his mind that the woman's instability might be cause for alarm before the evening was over.

He checked the gold, diamond-encrusted Rolex on his wrist.

It was ten minutes past ten.

Well, he thought, *let's see what the KGB man has to offer.*

The rear gardens were terraced down the hill at the rear of the villa. From the flat pool area by the house they extended about a hundred yards to a high but scalable wall.

Carter found the bodyguard crumpled in a darkened corner of the wall. The routine was fairly obvious. Some sound, probably in another part of the garden, had lured him from the villa. A 9mm Beretta was lying a foot from the body.

Carter sniffed the barrel. It had never been fired.

The kill was very professional, quick and clean. The Killmaster could spot it in an instant. He had used it many times in the past: left arm around the neck and chest, a stiletto just under the right ear, the point thrust up into the brain. Hardly a drop of blood, and no sound.

The guard had probably never even gotten a glance at the man who killed him.

Using his own penlight, Carter checked the mashed-down area where the killer had waited. Evidently he had been there for some time, probably since the first advent of darkness.

Returning to the villa, he crisscrossed the garden several times until he was satisfied that there had been only one attacker and he was long gone.

Back inside, he found that Noreen Parris had pulled herself together. She was going from room to room wiping surfaces with a dish towel.

"Just what the hell are you doing?" Carter barked.

"Getting rid of his fingerprints. I can't have this connected to me. The villa is rented in my name."

Carter exploded. "*What?*"

"You heard me; the villa is rented in my name. I rented it from Cyprus before we left."

She moved to a second bedroom and Carter followed. "You said it was a friend's villa—that you just borrowed it."

She stopped, glanced once at Carter, and shrugged. "I lied. I didn't think anyone could follow us to Bahrain. The country isn't that easy to get into."

There was a half-empty bag on the floor beside the bed. She hoisted it to the bed and started filling it with men's clothes from a nearby bureau.

"Damn Quentin! I told him not to leave Nanwandu alone for a minute," she muttered. "He's probably gone down the hill for a packet of those filthy cigars he smokes."

"Who's Quentin?"

"Quentin Collis, the bodyguard I told you I hired in London."

"Quentin's dead, lady," Carter growled. "I just found him down at the end of the garden. Somebody stuck a stiletto into his brain."

Noreen Parris stopped packing the bodyguard's bag and faced Carter squarely. Her face was emotionless, her eyes flat. The Killmaster could not begin to read her thoughts.

"It's his own fault," she said at last. "Obviously he wasn't as good as he said he was."

Carter remembered Maury Richland's recent words in the hotel room: ". . . her stud, a guy named Collis."

The lady was cold.

The Killmaster's balled fist hit her dead center in the pit of the stomach. Every ounce of air left her lungs, and her eyes widened in sudden shock. The force of the blow lifted her completely over one of the twin beds and deposited her between them.

Carter went right over the bed after her. She lay, both hands around her gut, her mouth gasping open and closed, vainly trying to suck air. She looked like a beached fish, or, in Carter's mind, a shark out of water.

"Don't move, lady, not even when you can. Just stay put and get everything in line. Because when I finish going through this dump in case your pal left anything I can use, you and I are going to sit down and I'm going to pick your brains."

He stormed through the villa until he found the kitchen. Once there, he rummaged until he found a pair of rubber gloves. When his hands were covered, he began a slow, thorough, meticulous search of every room.

FOUR

With all the guests inside, the two marine guards at the door and the one at the gate were able to relax. They thought nothing of the tall, beautiful black girl dressed in flowing apron and skirt coming around the end of the house.

They did think it slightly odd when she smiled and nodded and moved between them into the darkness of the entryway in front of the door.

Why is she coming from the rear of the house and entering through the front door?

But they merely exchanged looks and shrugged, until they heard the low, ominous tone in her voice and her words.

"We are taking over the legation. No, don't either of you move, not yet. The rest of my people are already inside. A wrong sound will cause someone's death. You, on the right, do you understand my English?"

The marine nodded.

"Turn your head, slowly, and look at me."

He did, and saw the ugly snout of an Uzi submachine gun slowly moving between himself and the other marine.

"I see it."

"Good. Call your comrade at the gate. Tell him to lock up and go around and fetch tea."

"He won't do it," the marine replied.

"He will. I have seen you do it several times."

The young marine swallowed, bit his lip, and called out, "Ho, Tom!"

"Yeah?"

"Lock her up for a bit and fetch a cuppa for us."

"Right you are."

The sound of the clanging gates echoed clearly across the compound, quickly followed by the marine's boots on the cobbled drive. But instead of going around to the rear of the villa, he was headed directly toward his two comrades and the black woman with the Uzi.

Inside the villa, small talk in the usual manner had been done away with. Introductions were made, and each of the four men sized up Hadj Bal-Sakiet.

For an Arab he looked more like the product of a lightless place. His skin was almost pale, and it looked as though even a few minutes—let alone most of a lifetime—in the harsh African sun would burn him to a crisp.

He was short of stature and powerfully built, with slightly pointed ears, as a child might have drawn the ears of an elf. The long face narrowed to a pointed chin of exaggerated length, and his eyes were set too close together. The whole was topped by coarse dark hair that was combed straight forward.

He had set the briefcase he had carried with him on the top of a round table and unsnapped the lid but kept it closed.

"Gentlemen, I assure you that in this briefcase you will find all the intelligence you will need to stop a juggernaut killing machine from rolling across the length and breadth of Africa and the Middle East.''

Hadj Bal-Sakiet was just lifting the lid when all hell
broke loose.

"You will all keep your positions and put your hands
behind your heads or you will be very dead!''

The speaker was a tall, huskily built man dressed in
black from his head to his feet. Even his hands holding a
submachine gun were encased in thin black gloves.

He had suddenly appeared from the adjacent dining
room. At the same time, two more black-hooded figures
slipped into the room, one from the study, the other
from the rear hallway.

Sir Martin was the first one to regain his wits. He
stepped forward and planted himself in front of the
hooded creature who had first spoken.

"See here, what is the meaning of this!''

The tall man stepped back a pace from the Englishman and mockingly gave him an imitation of the
three-point Arab genuflection of respect—heart, lips,
and forehead.

"A thousand pardons, Sir Martin Ramsey, but it
means that this house and all those in it are now under
our control.''

"Be damned if it is!'' Sir Martin roared. "I'll not
have another Khartoum here . . .''

Later, Sir Martin would say that he only meant to use
words; he merely wanted to try to get on a level with the
hooded terrorists so they wouldn't have so much in-
timidation when the time for the inevitable bargaining
arrived.

But as he stepped toward the man, Sir Martin's toe
caught on the edge of the rug. He tripped, and the terrorist mistook it for an attack.

He whirled the butt of the Uzi around, smashing it
into Sir Martin's face. Bones cracked and blood spurted
from the Britisher's nose and a deep gash in his cheek.

He melted to the floor, completely unconscious.

But the trip and the blow served as a catalyst to the others in the room.

Sylvia Ramsey's mind, awash in gin, could not reason out properly what her eyes saw. All she could think of when she saw the butt of the Uzi smash her husband's face was death.

On instinct alone, she snatched the small chrome pistol from her bag. She held it directly in front of her face and began to fire point-blank at her attacker.

Almost simultaneously, gunfire erupted in the front of the building and the ugly snout of a shotgun slammed through the glass in the French doors to the rear of the room.

A .22-caliber pistol is a toy compared to other small arms, but at the short range it was being used in Lady Sylvia's hands it became very deadly. By the time the firing pin had clicked on empty, five of the pistol's six slugs had crashed into Adee Milnai's chest.

She was standing over the black-clad terrorist, her finger trying to coax more bullets from the empty pistol, when a blast from the shotgun hit her dead center in the back.

The only sound she emitted was a surprised gasp as the force of the pellets threw her across the room.

She died as her body hit the floor like a bloody rag doll.

At the same time, Oranomi burst into the room, prodding two of the marines in front of her with the barrel of the Uzi. One of them held a shattered left arm to his side.

Thus far, the operation had taken less than a minute, so fast that the two Americans, Fischer and Wright, were frozen in place. Musalam Al-Sir was also shocked into stunned immobility. And Bal-Sakiet, the KGB defector, was moving, but not fast enough. When the shotgun had blasted Sylvia Ramsey, he had moved toward the door only to be brought up short by one of the other two terrorists with an Uzi.

When Oranomi saw her husband on the floor, blood pumping from his chest, her first instinct was to scream and turn the Uzi she held on the others in the room. But it took only seconds for her training to calm her.

"Cover these two!" she barked, and dropped to Molnai's side.

He was breathing raggedly, but his eyes, open and staring up at her, were alert. "How do we stand?"

"I had to kill the gate marine," she replied, her voice calm, "and wound another. But the building is ours."

"Lean closer." She did, putting her ear to his lips so he could whisper. "You must carry on, Oranomi. The demands . . . in my back pocket."

Gently she pulled an envelope from his rear pocket. "I have them."

"Remember the instructions. Burn the contents of the briefcase . . ."

"And kill Bal-Sakiet. I know."

"But it must look as though his is a random death."

"Don't talk anymore. We'll get a doctor." She stood and whirled to face the others. "You, Al-Sir!"

"Yes."

"Here are our demands!" She whipped a typed sheet of paper from the envelope and thrust it at the sheik.

He scanned it and looked up. "Odd."

"What do you mean?"

"The ransom of cash you demand I can understand, but the prisoners you want freed . . ."

"What about them?"

"They are from practically every revolutionary group. And they are all leaders, in most cases paid assassins. The countries holding them will never release them. These are impossible demands. They will never be met."

"Then the others here will die, one by one. Go, in-form the world that they have twelve hours. Then we will start shooting them, one by one!''

Al-Sir looked at the two Americans and then back to the woman. ''As the representative of this country—''

Her hand whipped out like a snake, lashing him across the face. ''Go! Now! And tell those outside that we want a doctor at once. Take him to the front gate and release him!''

One of the men with an Uzi stepped forward and prodded Musalam Al-Sir from the room.

''The rest of you, down below, into the wine cellar!''

The two Americans, Fischer and Wright, moved toward the hall. Hadj Bal-Sakiet followed them, plucking his briefcase from the table in passing.

''Leave that!'' Oranomi hissed, emphasizing her command with the Uzi.

He paused, biting his lip and gazing longingly down at the briefcase that held his only lifeline to the West. But when she barked the command again, he hastily dropped it and followed the two Americans.

The man with the shotgun stepped through the French windows. ''They have arrived, the army. The legation is surrounded.''

''They will do nothing for twelve hours,'' Oranomi replied, opening the briefcase and emptying the contents on the table. ''Help me!''

Together, they shredded the papers and dropped them into a metal wastebasket. When it was almost full, the woman lit a match and they watched the papers burn.

''Tell Obar to separate Bal-Sakiet from the two Americans. We don't want him talking.''

The man nodded and rushed from the room. Oranomi knelt by her husband's side and felt for his pulse. It was there, but weak. His eyes were closed. She lifted one eyelid and stared into the eye.

He was alive, but she knew it would be only a matter of time.

It took well over an hour for Carter to go through each room of the villa. He finally found something that didn't fit, in the back bedroom that the bodyguard, Collis, had been using.

There was a single window overlooking the rear garden. There were drapes and sheers over the window. The continuous cord on the drapes was intact. There were two single pull cords on the sheers; one was a good deal shorter than the other. It had been cut and the little plastic pull had been awkwardly reattached.

Carter struggled with the window. It was hard to open, but after a few minutes of banging with the heel of his hand it loosened and slid upward.

Hide in plain sight, Carter thought.

One end of the cord was tied to a stout length of bougainvillaea vine. It trailed down through the vines and blossoms to a small chamois bag.

Carter untied the bag, left the cord hanging, and headed back toward the front bedroom.

Noreen Parris hadn't followed orders. She had moved and moved a lot since his departure from the room. The closet behind an open door was empty and the drawers of a single dresser were pulled out. There was an open bag beside the bed, stuffed with the contents of the dresser drawers and the closet.

The woman stood on one foot in front of the vanity mirror. She was leaning forward, her other foot resting on the low stool while she carefully drew a stocking upward over her shapely ankle and calf. The other leg was already stockinged and attached to a narrow lacy garter belt.

She wore nothing else.

"I didn't know women still wore those things."

"I do," she replied without a quiver of emotion in her voice. "It's cooler than wearing pantyhose."

Carter's gaze flickered from her naked ass to the bag, to the grotesque, wide-eyed corpse on the bed.

Everything about this woman, Carter thought, was cool. In fact, ice cold.

"Just what the hell do you think you're doing?" he growled.

"What does it look like I'm doing? I'm dressing and packing."

She straightened slowly as the stocking came the rest of the way up. As she snapped it in place, Carter moved around to face her and dropped the chamois bag on the vanity table top.

"Ever see this before?"

She stared, eyes wide and round. "Yes, he always wore it on a gold chain around his neck."

Carter glanced at the corpse. The gold chain was still around his neck. Noreen was reaching for the bag. Carter stopped her.

"Allow me."

He opened the drawstring and tipped the bag. A passport, a ring, a key, and a wad of bills held together by a rubber band spilled out.

Again her hand slipped forward. The Killmaster slapped her wrist.

"Naughty, naughty."

The money was American, all hundreds, about four thousand dollars' worth.

The passport was South African, issued to Abu Pastomau. It carried only one entry and exit stamp and Nanwandu's picture. Obviously, it was the one he had used for the aborted kill on the priest in Johannesburg. The dead man had probably kept it as a last-ditch escape valve, in case others screwed him the way the Russian had done.

Carter held it up to the mirror and the light. It was a

good forgery, but nevertheless a fake.

"He was wearing that ring when I first met him."

"You mean when Maury Richland brought you to him in Cyprus," Carter said, picking up the ring.

Out of the corner of his eye he could see a little color fading from her face. Other than that, she kept her cool and slid a lightweight summer dress over her head. It slithered down her body. Her eyes, when they emerged, weren't looking at the ring Carter held. They were staring intently at the key still on the tabletop.

Carter picked it up. "Ever see this before?"

"No," she replied, quickly moving to the suitcase.

"You're lying."

"I'm not," she said, slipping her feet into a few straps that served as shoes.

"What does it fit?"

She shrugged and closed the suitcase.

Carter grabbed her by the shoulders, straightened her, and turned her until her nose was almost touching his chin.

"Look, lady, we don't play the game the same way, and your way is stupid. Maury Richland put you together with this stiff because he needed a banker. You double-crossed Maury. My guess is, it was because he wanted to turn the guy over to MI6, and you knew they would cut you out. So you go to our State Department where you think you've got friends. Only you find out they don't send some candy-ass out here, they send me. And I don't like your crap. Then you try to make like an amateur James Bond and you get your boy killed . . ."

He paused, out of breath.

"You through?" she asked, unruffled.

"Almost," he replied, dragging her across the room and seating her on the vanity stool. "Now, I want to know everything you know."

Her ice blue eyes returned his stare as the little cogs in her mind whirled. Carter could almost read her mental printout as it clicked to the surface.

At last she started talking.

"As I told you, they call themselves the One Hundred Eyes. It comes from the original one hundred faithful members of the group. It was formed several years ago by one man."

"Who?"

"I don't know. But Nanwandu told me that their aim is African unity, the whole continent under the rule of the cult."

"Or the one-man leader."

She nodded. "Most likely. He has built himself a fortress somewhere. That's another thing Nanwandu wouldn't tell me."

"And they have financed themselves through terrorism."

"Yes," she said. "At first it was only for money. Now it's for influence. They use kidnapping and blackmail to influence certain governments' positions in their favor."

She stopped and lifted the ring from his fingers. The setting was a bloodstone, bright red. As Carter watched, she depressed the stone and turned it. Under it was a concave flatness, empty.

"He showed me this," she said, handing it to Carter. "Hold it up to the light."

The Killmaster moved around her, lifted the ring, and placed the opening against his eye.

Immediately he saw what resembled a night sky festooned with little golden stars. As his eye became more acclimated, he could see that the stars were eyes, slanted like a cat's, with bright red slits for pupils.

"A hundred eyes," Carter murmured.

"Yes," Noreen replied. "He said the rings serve two purposes. One is identification. The other has something to do with codes."

Carter put the ring back to his eye.

It could be a cipher key, he thought, *the way the eyes are grouped.* It wasn't much, but at least it was a start.

He reset the bloodstone and pocketed the ring along with the money and the passport. The key he palmed and held before her face.

"What about the key?"

She looked from his hand up to his eyes, but said nothing.

"Well?"

"I've never seen it before. But I've got a pretty good idea where it's from."

Carter leaned his face close to hers. "What's your 'pretty good idea'?"

"I'll tell you—for a trade."

Carter straightened, his face like a rock, his eyes hooded and coldly menacing. "I told you, no more games."

"I want an exclusive on what that key brings."

Carter didn't have to think. "Deal. You would have gotten that anyway."

"And I want you to help me get these bodies away from the villa. I don't want them connected to me."

Carter put both hands on her shoulders and leaned forward until his face was inches from hers. "You were dumb enough to rent the villa in your own name. You clean up the mess. I don't have time."

"Then you chase the lock that goes with the key."

His fingers tightened roughly on her shoulders. His voice was low and hoarse, charged with the passion of anger. "What do I have to do to prove to you that I'm not a nice man? This obviously fits a locker or storage container of some kind."

Noreen Parris did not flinch from the hurting pressure of his fingers. Her eyes were wide now, and shining. Her lips parted as the breath came in and out more swiftly.

He knew by instinct that she wouldn't crack under

threats. He also knew that with her clout he could only push so far.

He set his teeth and let go of her shoulders with a little shove that sent her back against the low dressing table. He turned and took a few steps across the room, and wheeled to face her at this safer distance.

"Okay, you've got a deal. What about the key?"

"No way. We clean this mess up and I lead you to it."

"I don't think you trust me," Carter quipped.

"No more than you trust me. I'll give you half. It's on Cyprus. Deal?"

"Yeah," Carter said, "deal. Finish wiping their prints off everything. I'll get the stiff out of the garden."

"Fields . . ."

"Yeah?"

"Give me half a break and I'll play square with you. All I want is the story."

"Okay, that's a deal too. But from here on in, we do everything my way."

FIVE

Carter's estimation of Noreen Parris's coolness went up several points as they wrapped the two bodies in the already blood-soaked bedding and carried them out to the Mercedes.

Her demeanor was calm, without the slightest trace of squeamishness, as they dropped them into the trunk and secured the lid.

"Now the bags."

She nodded and followed him back into the villa. Fifteen minutes later the bags were loaded and Carter was on the phone to the airport. There were ample seats on the night flight to Athens, with a good morning connection to the international airport at Larnaca on Cyprus.

Carter held his hand over the mouthpiece. "Are you traveling on your own passport?"

Noreen looked dumbfounded. "Yes, of course."

He smiled. "Some of us don't always."

She understood, and yet another flush suffused her face. He made two reservations in the names of N. Fields and N. Parris and hung up.

"What does the *N* stand for?"

"Nick," he replied, hoisting her bag and heading for the Mercedes.

"I don't support Fields is your real name."

"No, I don't suppose it is." He deposited the luggage in the back seat of the Mercedes and tossed her the keys to his rental. "You drive mine, and stay close."

"I'm ready whenever you are," she replied. "Which direction are you taking?"

"Back toward Manama. I noticed a deep ravine on the inland side, just before we reach the corniche."

She nodded. "Okay."

As she passed Carter while walking to the Audi, moonlight fell across her face. It revealed the opposite mood from the calmness in her voice.

As the old cliché goes, Noreen Parris looked a little green around the gills.

Carter swung the Mercedes around until the long hood faced the entrance gates. He had to wait until a car sped past from the direction of Manama and the gulf before he nosed out and headed the way the car had come. In the rearview mirror he saw the lights of the Audi as it swung out and fell in behind him.

He pushed the big car up to about fifty. The road was too twisting and narrow to travel much faster, even though the Killmaster had a gut urge to move and get out of the country as fast as possible.

A quick glance told him that Noreen was keeping pace.

And then he saw them, another pair of lights about two hundred yards behind the Audi, keeping pace with Noreen.

Carter slowed, took one hand from the wheel, and unholstered the Luger. He put the gun in his lap and slowed some more as they hit a long stretch of straight road.

Noreen crawled up on his rear bumper and, to Carter's relief, the lights behind her kept coming. He could see Noreen's head and shoulders outlined against the rocking glare of the lights behind her.

Seconds later, there was the blare of a horn and the last car pulled out to pass. Carter drove with this left hand and rested the barrel of the Luger in his right hand on his left elbow.

It was a small green Fiat, driver and one passenger, both white, male. Carter watched them carefully, but they both stayed intent on the road and sped on past the Mercedes.

The Killmaster waited until the taillights of the Fiat disappeared before he sped up, at the same time relaxing and sliding the Luger back into its sheath under his left armpit.

The road twisted around the face of a hill, and then off to the right, far below, were the lights of the beach and the villas lining it. Ahead, far in the distance, was the glow in the sky above Manama.

About a half mile short of the corniche, he spotted an opening to his left and stopped. Noreen slowed behind him and came to a halt. Carter backed into the turnoff as far as he could and got out. She pulled the Audi directly in front of the Mercedes.

She started to get out.

"I can handle it," he said.

"No," she said resolutely, and joined him at the rear of the car.

Together they muscled the bodies from the trunk and tipped them over the lip of rock and soft dirt. They heard the crunching sounds for only a few seconds, and then silence.

"How deep is it?" she asked.

"Deep enough, and probably rocky. They won't be found for days."

"What about the bedding?" she asked.

"What about it?"

"Won't they trace it?"

"Honey, this isn't Manhattan," Carter said dryly. "They don't have hotshot NYPD forensics here. And, besides, those aren't two natives down there. Collis, being an Englishman, might raise some questions, but by then we'll be long gone."

"Are you always so ruthless?"

"Always. Aren't you?" He tossed the bags. "Let's go."

They drove directly to the Vendôme, where Carter turned in the Audi, explaining to Noreen that they would use the Mercedes to get to the airport.

They were just getting into the elevator when Carter spotted the driver of the little green Fiat sitting at the end of the hotel bar. From that position, the man could see the front entrance and the elevators.

Coincidence? Carter wondered.

He didn't think so.

They stepped out of the elevator on the fifth floor into a crescendo of sound. The door to the suite at the end of the hall was open. Beyond it was a noisy party. The chatter of conversation in three or four different languages, loud music, and now and then shrill laughter filled the hall.

Carter was at the door of his own suite, key in hand, when a tall, overweight woman dripping diamonds and sporting what could only be described as orange hair stepped into the doorway and eyed Carter with a leering smile.

Carter didn't return the smile, and fit the key into the lock. At the last second, he remembered Maury Richland's boozy state and the Webley that was cradled in his lap. Maury would probably be touchy.

Carter knocked.

There was no reply.

"Is somebody here with you?" Noreen asked at his side.

Carter didn't reply, and shoved the door open.

The lights were on, blazing across the rumpled bed. Both empty whiskey bottles were in the middle of the bed, with a note propped up between them.

It didn't take a genius to see that the ex-MI6 man had flown.

Noreen moved in beside him and Carter closed the door. He had underestimated Richland's capacity. Obviously, the man could be dead drunk and still think and move.

Carter moved to the bed and snatched up the note. He could sense the woman at his shoulder reading it along with him, but didn't bother to stop her.

You've been made, palley, You got a hardcase phone call and they were speaking to Carter, not Fields. The guy spoke English with a hard Volga accent. I tried to string him, but he figured I wasn't you. Thought I'd better vacate in case they came for a look-see. If they want your ass, I didn't want them finding mine. I can be reached through the old Sievers contact in Berlin . . . say 24 hours. Don't cross me, palley. M.

"Maury Richland," Noreen whispered. "That's how you knew."

"Right," Carter growled. "I tried to keep him on ice, in case he knew more than you did."

He slipped the note into his pocket and started filling his bag from the dresser and closet.

"Nanwandu might have told Richland more than he told me. Maury was with him for almost two weeks before he contacted me."

Carter slipped the Luger's rig into the false bottom of the suitcase and unstrapped a chamois sheath from his right forearm.

"What's that?" Noreen asked.

The Killmaster tensed the muscles of his arm, gave a twitch, and a thin, deadly stiletto shot into his right palm.

"I call it Hugo. Your boyfriend, Collis, bought it with one just like it."

"Ugly," Noreen mumbled, and turned away.

"Beauty is in the eye of the beholder," Carter mused, sliding the stiletto back into its sheath and stowing it with the Luger. "Come on, we've got an hour to catch a plane."

"You have eight hours, no more. If our demands are not met at that time, we will kill the first hostage. And I will accept no more phone calls from the outside."

Oranomi replaced the phone and turned to the hooded man beside her.

"Why don't we just kill the Russian and bargain our escape with the other three?" he asked her.

"You know we can't do that," she replied. "It must look like the demands are legitimate and Bal-Sakiet was killed as a hostage."

"But Adee . . ."

The name was barely out of his mouth when another of their comrades stepped into the room with a tall, gaunt, gray-haired man at his side. The man was an English doctor they had sent in from the street.

"How is he?" Oranomi asked anxiously.

"Gone," the doctor replied.

She cursed with a wailing scream and slammed the side of her fist so hard on the table that glasses skittered to the floor.

The doctor rocked back in alarm, fearful that her angry outburst would prompt her comrades to seek instant revenge on him.

Only after several minutes did he feel safe enough to venture further speech. "If I don't get Sir Martin

Ramsey to hospital soon, I am afraid his face will be beyond repair . . .''

The tall black woman started to blow again. With trembling hands she snatched the Uzi from the table in front of her and whirled the barrel around toward the doctor.

At the last second, she regained her composure, lifted the weapon, and settled the sling over her shoulder.

"Take the wounded Englishman, the doctor, and the dead woman out to the gates."

"But, Oranomi—"

"Do it!" she cried, and stalked into the adjoining bedroom to bid a silent good-bye to her dead husband.

It happened on a narrow stretch of dark road about halfway between Manama and the airport. Noreen was driving, with Carter deep in thought beside her.

He was alerted when the big, steel gray sedan moved up on their left and kept abreast of them for several seconds before moving ahead. There were two men in front, both dressed in traditional Arab robes.

What clinched it was the headlights coming up hard behind them. He'd seen them before. Though he couldn't see the color or make of the car behind them, Carter was pretty sure it was a green Fiat.

"Stop!"

"What?"

"Stop, now!" Carter hissed, cursing himself for putting the Luger in his bag before they reached the airport.

It was too late. The driver of the big sedan had executed a perfect brodie in front of them, effectively blocking the road. Carter had no doubts that the Fiat behind them was prepared to make the same move.

Noreen had to floor the brake and go into a slide herself to avoid slamming headlong into the sedan.

Carter rolled out of the car, hoping that a surprise attack would counter what looked like a foolproof plan.

The two from the sedan had the same idea, and the Killmaster could already hear the pounding feet coming up from the Fiat.

As the two from the sedan got closer, they separated, coming in on both sides of him very professionally. Carter chanced a look, quickly, over his shoulder. The two men were out of the Fiat and almost to the front doors of the Mercedes.

"Noreen!" Carter shouted. "Lock the doors and drive!"

The words were scarcely out of his mouth before he lashed out at the closest one to him, connecting solid with the side of the man's neck with a chop.

Caught by surprise, the man tried to back off. He avoided most of the impact, but took a stinging slice across his cheek.

Number two was holding his hands up, palms out. "Talk, American, just talk!" the man rasped, backing up.

"Talk, shit," Carter growled, butting the man's face with his head and just missing an elbow to the center of the gut.

Now both of them tossed talk to the winds and started circling. Carter was ready, but the attack came with such blinding speed, such animal ferocity, that it sent him reeling and staggering onto the grass of the median.

Somewhere he heard glass smashing. Something exploded against the side of his head. He heard a grunt of exertion, a hissing inhalation of breath. He went down on one knee on the wet grass and came up against a big, shadowy shape that loomed over him.

He smelled stale booze and fish on the man's breath. A pale trench coat flapped in the wind. Carter rammed his shoulder against a solid belly that felt more like oak than a man's flesh. Another grunt, and something slashed at his head, hammering pain down his spine.

Carter came up a second time, felt a trickle of blood

against his temple, ducked the next blow, and slammed his fist against the round, dimly seen face of the big man. He connected obliquely; there was a mumble of surprise, and again a stale waft of fish in his face. The man staggered slightly . . . as much as an oak in a summer breeze.

"Enough!" a voice shouted somewhere in the rear, and Noreen called Carter's name in a shrill but oddly muffled voice.

Carter managed to stagger to one knee and stare toward the Mercedes through the blood seeping into his eyes.

The pair from the Fiat had smashed out the driver's side window of the Mercedes and unlocked the door. Now one of them was holding Noreen in a death grip around the throat, with his knee in the small of her back.

Carter knew the hold. He had used it many times himself to throttle a lot of people.

But so what, he thought. Noreen Parris was a bitch. Why should he stop fighting just because they threatened to croak her?

He opened his mouth to shout "Waste her!"—but nothing came out.

Instead, he flopped over on his face in the grass and passed out.

SIX

Rather than sound the hour with a clamor, the large
Swiss-made clock on the wall announced it with a barely
perceptible *ding*. The clock, like its British master, was
reserved and conservative.

"It is time. Bring them up from the cellar, and watch
yourselves. If Bal-Sakiet gets any indication of what's in
store for him, he might try something. He is sly and he is
fast."

The three men adjusted the black hoods over their
faces, took up their arms, and left the room.

The black woman slowly surveyed the opulence of the
room as she waited. There were huge couches, over-
stuffed and covered with pillows. A handsome oriental
carpet covered the center of the floor, and a glass-and-
chrome coffee table, imported from Europe, held price-
less antiquities.

From where she stood, near a large teak sideboard
that served as a bar, Oranomi looked through a large
picture window and across a wide terrace to the lights of
Salala along the shore.

Had Adee survived, she thought, the two of them
would have lived like this one day, in wealth and com-
fort.

Suddenly she shrugged and turned to the bar.

It was not meant to be.

She poured a large snifter of brandy, and from a pocket produced a generous pinch of finely ground hashish. She stirred the drug into the brandy, and just as she was about to drink, the telephone rang.

"Yes?"

"This is Commander Gaylord Childress, head of the Omani garrison."

"The deadline has been passed."

"We know that," the Britisher said, tension in his voice. "I must speak to the one in charge. I am afraid we have a large impasse."

"You are speaking to the person in charge, Commander." Oranomi paused, waiting for a reply. When none came, she spoke again. "Yes, a woman, Commander. Now, what is it? I am very busy."

"Do you have a name?"

"Names are unimportant," she replied coldly. "Your time is up."

"I know that, but you must realize that we are dealing with governments of five different countries here, and we have practically no diplomatic relations with two of them. Not only are your demands unreasonable, they are practically impossible!"

"That is your problem, Commander."

"I beg you, give us more time."

Oranomi heard the group, hostages and guards, enter the room behind her, and hung up. She took a long drink of brandy and turned to face them.

Albert Fischer, one of the two Americans, stepped forward. "I would like to contact Wash—"

It was all he got out before the barrel of the woman's Uzi smashed into his belly.

"Take the two Americans into the drawing room, there. Odo, take this Arab-Russian pig into the front sitting room!"

The youngest of the terrorists nodded and prodded

Bal-Sakiet with his shotgun. His eyes in the slits of his hood were glassy, as were those of his two male comrades. All three of them had shared a powerful pipe of hashish in the process of fetching the prisoners.

Thus far, the KGB man had not been able to put the whole picture together. But passing the still smoldering wastebasket and his open, empty briefcase told him what he had already suspected.

These were not just ordinary terrorists. They were not from any established or even splinter group. They were members of the One Hundred Eyes, and they had been sent for the express purpose of silencing him.

The terrorist behind him was young, just a boy. He was probably highly trained, as all of them were, but not experienced.

Out of the corner of his eye he saw the two Americans disappear with their guards into the study. The woman stayed, sipping her brandy and glaring at him with obvious hatred in her dark eyes.

He moved down the hall, weighing his chances. The front sitting room was small. There was a straight-backed chair just inside the door. He had noticed the layout when he had entered earlier.

"In there!" the boy said, guiding with the double barrels of the shotgun.

Bal-Sakiet nodded and turned into the room. Just inside the door, he rolled the chair into the boy's path and whirled at the same time. His right fist thudded into the young man's head just above the left ear.

Between the chair and the blow, the young terrorist momentarily lost his composure. Instead of firing the shotgun, he thrust it forward like a club to ward off his attacker. But a second blow caught him full in the face as the shotgun was wrenched from his hands.

Reeling from the blow, the boy pushed himself from the wall to form a perfect target for a swift foot to the chest. He went down hard to the sound of running feet in the hallway.

Instantly, the KGB agent looked for some sort of cover in the room. His initial plan had been to disarm the boy and dive through the large front windows. But they had shuttered the windows, making that avenue of escape impossible.

It would be only seconds before . . .

The boy threw himself across the floor, trying to grasp Bal-Sakiet's ankles. The man turned, kicking at the grasping hands.

Too late, Bal-Sakiet realized that he shouldn't have let the boy distract him. The burst of fire from the doorway told him that, as did the searing, shooting pains all along the left side of his body.

He whirled the shotgun toward the doorway.

It was the woman, jamming another magazine into the Uzi.

The machine gun chattered in tandem with the roaring shotgun.

Bal-Sakiet and the black woman fell forward to the floor, their heads nearly touching in death.

In seconds, the other two hooded figures filled the doorway. The boy lurched to his feet, his whole body quaking.

"She's dead! The bastard has killed her!" he cried. "What do we do now?"

The larger of the other two men, his eyes calm in the slits of his hood, immediately took command.

"We continue with the plan. Oranomi is dead. So be it. We all face death to carry out the grand plan."

"But—" the boy croaked.

"No buts, comrade," the man said, his voice like ice. "Drag this pile of dung out to the front gates. I will cover you. We wait one hour and then negotiate our release, trading the two Americans for transportation and safety. Move!"

SEVEN

Carter awoke amid a profusion of antiseptic smells, the feel of an unfamiliar bed, and the sound of voices. At first they just droned, but soon his ears adjusted to words.

There were two of them, one male, one female, and they were speaking Russian.

"He's coming around."

"How bad is it?"

"A very slight concussion. He will have a headache for a few days. Beyond that, very little."

The man chuckled. "He has a very hard head. I know that from experience."

The Killmaster felt smothered, his face deep in a pillow. Why the hell was he on his stomach? He never slept on his stomach. He tried to move, but nothing happened.

Russians.

Maury Richland had said the voice on the phone had spoken with a strong Volga accent.

"Carter?" It was the male voice, bass and smoke-booze husky.

It was an effort even to open his eyes, but he forced the lids apart by sheer willpower.

63

Light flickered into his brain, and then an image. The image appeared to be a woman in a very baggy tweed jacket and slacks. Her face was plain and her figure nonexistent.

"Who are you?" Carter asked in Russian.

"Dr. Ludka Yakov. Let me welcome you back to the living, American."

"I can't move."

"Your ankles and wrists have been secured so you couldn't turn over in your sleep and start the bleeding again."

"My head hurts and my back burns."

"Your head hurts because you fought our people instead of giving them time to explain."

"Screw your people."

She ignored the comment. "Your back burns because you scraped a goodly amount of skin from it when you fell."

"I'll just bet I 'fell'," Carter grunted, guessing that the team of goons had dragged instead of carried him to the car after knocking him out. "Where am I?"

"You are aboard the fishing trawler *Smoldosk*, just outside the territorial waters off Bahrain."

It was the man's voice, familiar.

When the woman stepped inside, Carter was able to put a face to the voice: a broad, Slavic face with a red-veined nose and piercing black beads for eyes.

His name was Mock—to be precise, Major General Kolack Ivanovich Mock—African affairs expert, First Directorate, KGB.

"You have the most interesting way of summoning me before your august presence, General," Carter said, and shifted his head slightly for a better view of his captor. His vision had cleared completely now, and he realized that he was in a ship's cabin that had been made over into a small but adequate infirmary.

The salt-and-pepper-topped head shook in time with the rotund belly as the beefy man erupted in laughter.

"It would seem so. But you must admit that you came much more easily the last time."

Mock's reference to the "last time" concerned an international conglomerate named Cyclops taking over the tiny African nation of Togo. And there would have been no Soviet-American cooperation then if Cyclops hadn't managed to boot the Soviets out of Togo in the process of their own attempted coup.

That time, there had been no goons on the grab, just a very beautiful woman.

Carter wondered if his current kidnapping was along the same lines . . . or worse. It was common knowledge in the business that Moscow had a very heavy price on his head. Had Mock and Company finally decided it was collection time?

"Am I on my way to Moscow, General?"

"Of course not, my boy, quite the contrary. How's your head?"

"Lousy."

"Unfasten the ties."

The woman stepped to Carter's side and went to work with her pudgy fingers. She wasn't gentle.

When she stepped back, Carter stretched—grimacing with pain. He wondered just how much skin remained on his back.

"Can you stand?" Mock asked.

Carter slid from the bed and stood on wobbly legs. "Stand, yes. Move? That's anybody's guess."

Mock hefted himself from the chair and, contrary to his size, moved like a cat to Carter's side.

"My cabin is next door. I suggest we move in there. I must say the antiseptic smell in here reminds me of my own mortality."

The arm around Carter's shoulder was solid, the grip steady. Mock might have been an overweight sixty, but he was hard as nails where it mattered.

The Russian practically shoved the dowdy female doctor out of the way and half carried Carter across the room and through the hatch.

"A little *zakuski*!" he exclaimed, arcing his arm over a well-filled table and slamming the hatch behind.

The Killmaster made his way alone to a soft leather chair and settled in, making sure he sat well forward to protect his back. Mock moved to the opposite side of the table and began filling a plate from the mound of appetizers spread between them.

Carter spotted several cheeses, smoked sturgeon, hard sausage, cold salmon, and white mushrooms. A chilled bottle of vodka sat near at hand by both chairs.

"Am I being softened up for the kill?" Carter asked dryly, pouring two glasses from the bottle nearest him.

"Hardly," Mock chortled. "If that had been my intent, you wouldn't be here. No, my friend, if I wanted you dead, I most assuredly would not bring you abroad a Soviet trawler to commit the deed."

Carter knew that to be true. For all of Mock's jovial nature, the man was a thorough technician. He did nothing without a good reason, and rarely made mistakes. He was also a party loyalist, which was why he had survived and risen to a fairly exalted status in the KGB heirarchy. The only way he would ever deter from the party line was to bend the rules to further the party line.

General Mock was one of the few, if not the only, KGB fieldman who rated high in the *Nomenklatura* hierarchy, the secret list of the party elite. And he hadn't reached that status by being soft or making mistakes in judgment.

Carter exchanged one of the glasses for a plate, and Mock raised it in a toast.

"To survival and your pension."

Carter smiled. "To high party salaries, a good Moscow apartment, *dachas*, government cars with chauffeurs, special railway cars, VIP treatment . . ."

"Enough, enough!" Mock laughed. "*Na zdorov'e!*"

"*Na zdorov'e*," Carter said.

They drank, then attacked their plates. The point was made. Carter, on his capitalist, imperialist salary, could never afford what a KGB officer of equal rank in the Soviet People's Society could achieve materially.

They ate in silence. When they were finished, Mock poured from an excellent bottle of brandy and opened a box of Havana cigars.

"These are about the only good things we get from Castro," he quipped.

When the cigars were lit and a sufficient amount of brandy sipped, Mock leaned back in his chair and his face assumed the stern mask of the Soviet negotiator. It was then Carter knew the reason he was on the trawler *Smoldosk*.

Major General Mock wanted some kind of a deal.

"The woman, Noreen Parris, is safe."

Carter shrugged. "The woman, Noreen Parris, is, as we say in the States, a pain in the ass."

Mock chuckled. "I have come to the same conclusion. We trailed her from Cyprus and you from Rome, hoping that it was you she was to contact."

"Oh?"

"Yes. You see, Carter, we wanted her to deliver Jabar Nanwandu to you."

Carter was somehow not surprised at this revelation. He guessed that Mock knew as much or more than he did. It wasn't a hard decision to toss something the Russian's way.

"Nanwandu's dead, garotted in the villa. I dumped the body."

"A pity." Here Mock paused and swung forward in the chair. "How much do you know of the One Hundred Eyes?"

"Only what I've learned from the Parris woman and what I've pieced together from guesswork, and that isn't much. The whole thing sounds a bit farfetched."

"It isn't, I assure you," Mock grunted. "It is all too real. You know Bal-Sakiet?"

"I know of him," Carter said. "One of your best people here in Africa."

"It was Hadj Bal-Sakiet whom I sent to debrief Nanwandu originally. In the process of that, I received thin reports, very little substance, but enough to advance the money to buy full disclosure."

"General, I know your man double-crossed Nanwandu. That's what drove him into Maury Richland's arms, and, in turn, to Noreen Parris."

Mock sighed, his teeth clamping harder on his cigar. "It would seem that Hadj Bal-Sakiet's political indoctrination was not as complete as I would have liked."

Pieces started falling into place in Carter's mind. "Bal-Sakiet defected?"

"We think so. The money was never paid to Nanwandu. It was deposited in a bank in Bahrain under one of Bal-Sakiet's aliases . . . one we supplied him with, by the way."

"But you don't know where he is now?"

"Oh, yes. Hadj Bal-Sakiet is quite dead. I am positive he was attempting to defect to the British in Oman. The U.K. legation was overrun with terrorists several hours ago. Bal-Sakiet and Sylvia Ramsey, the U.K. representative's wife, were killed. On the surface, it would appear to be just another terrorist attack."

"But you don't think so."

"Not at all. I think the woman's death was an accident. I think Bal-Sakiet was the target. My guess is he was here to trade the Nanwandu information for asylum."

"And the One Hundred Eyes knew it."

"Exactly. There were five terrorists in the group. Two of them, a man and woman, were killed. The three that were left traded the lives of two of your State Department people who were in the legation for their escape."

Now Carter's face turned to stone and lightened a few shades. Mock didn't miss it.

"Two of our State Department people?" Carter said between clenched teeth.

"I know," Mock replied. "Depressing, isn't it? Bureaucracies in your country are just like bureaucracies in mine. Too damned often they fail to work together. It is possible that they didn't know the full details of what Nanwandu was willing to trade, but I doubt it. I rather think it was a case of two of your young Turks looking to score a coup for themselves."

Carter leaned forward until his face was just inches from the older man's. "Just what do you want, General? Why don't we simply lay it out on the table?"

The Russian took a long time, enough to pour two more glasses of brandy and relight his mangled cigar.

"For various reasons, I cannot actively—or I should say openly—pursue the leadership of this One Hundred Eyes. Nor can any agents of our Warsaw Pact allies—"

"Because you and your chums in the Bulgarian DS and the Czech StB have used these bastards yourself."

Mock took a long drag on his cigar and blew the smoke in a steady stream toward the overhead light. Carter had seen the stance many times. It was the perfect picture of the Soviet diplomat at the U.N. or in various disarmament talks, when the line was deafness or silence, mum's the word, to any criticism.

Carter wouldn't let it go.

"But they crossed you up, didn't they, General. They didn't play any favorites. They hit some of your people, didn't they . . . Probably people we don't know about."

The senior KGB man's eyes returned slowly to Carter's. The Killmaster could sense the inner turmoil going on within the man's mind, the decision he must make.

"It's up to you, General. In for a penny, in for a pound," Carter said, rolling the brandy in his glass.

"Between us?" Mock said at last, a growling sigh rumbling from deep within his barrel chest.

"Between us," Carter answered. "I've nothing to lose at this point."

From another drawer in his desk Mock withdrew a thin sheaf of papers and passed them across to Carter. Across the top, in bold red letters, was the Russian phrase for top secret, *sovershenno sekretnoe*.

"Needless to say, should word get back to Dzerzhinsky Square that I allowed you to read that, I would receive a *strogach* that would be fatal."

"And I, General, would myself receive a 'severe reprimand' for not reporting what I've read. 'Nuf said."

It was exactly as Carter had guessed. If anything, the Soviets had been hit as hard or harder than the West. There were fourteen occurrences involving sixteen deaths in Soviet-controlled or semicontrolled areas, mostly in Africa.

Carter scanned through it, and, to his surprise, when he handed it back Mock was chuckling.

"As I am sure you know, the life of one of our diplomats or my agents in Black Africa is difficult as it is. Add the threat of assassination, and it gets impossible to post people here from home."

Carter nodded and smiled himself. He knew that Africa was the armpit of the Soviet foreign ministry. Soviet diplomats in Angola, Somalia, Ethiopia, and countless other African nations leaning toward Marxism were so poorly supplied by Moscow that their families at home had to ship them foodstuffs. Expanding the Soviet presence in Black Africa was no picnic.

Mock moved a second sheet toward Carter, this one in bold print. It was in an African dialect with which Carter was unfamiliar. A typed translation was placed beside it.

It was a well-written propaganda sheet exhorting the native blacks to overthrow the superpower aggressors of both the U.S. and Russia. "The day will come," it said, "when Africa—all of Africa—will be ours!"

It went on in the same vein, and was signed by Ala-Din Muhammed, Grand Vizier, The Order of the One Hundred Eyes.

Carter looked up from the paper. "They've come out in the open."

"Yes, it would appear that they now have the finances and the power to make their move openly. We intercepted tons of these leaflets going all over the southern part of Africa. *This* time, we intercepted them. The next time they might very well get through."

Carter shrugged and tossed the paper back across the desk. "Maybe we should just let 'em swing," he said. "It would be one way of getting you booted out of Africa."

"True," the big Russian replied. "But I think it goes further than that. I think this maniac wants to control *all* of Africa. By that I mean the whole continent, from Casablanca to Alexandria to Cape Town."

"Impossible."

"Of course it is," Mock replied, standing now and beginning to pace the small cabin, his cigar breathing a constant wreath of smoke about his head. "But in the attempt, a goodly portion of the population could be decimated, and intertribal strife reactivated to the point where Africa could be a wasteland for the next one hundred years."

"Who is this Ala-Din Muhammed?"

Mock shrugged. "It is an adopted name, a symbol, if you will. As to the real identity, we have a few leads but nothing concrete. I will try to explain . . . that is, if you are willing to listen."

Carter, deep in thought, mashed out his own cigar. "So what's your proposition?"

"I don't have one, officially."

Suddenly it was all clear. "You mean to tell me you're doing this on your own?"

It was unheard of. Mock departing from official Moscow? Taking a situation under his own wing without informing his party superiors or abiding by their decisions?

The Russian returned to his desk, a pained expression on his face, his eyes dull. Carter had to force himself to accept the transition.

"I warned the Center over two years ago that, by using this group, we were only infecting our own sores."

"But they didn't listen."

"They are not listening even now."

"Jesus," Carter muttered, slumping painfully back in the chair and feeling the sweat pop out on his back to dampen his shirt.

He knew exactly what Mock was getting at without having the man spell it out. It was a cornerstone of Marxist-Leninist philosophy . . . confusion, turning neighbor against neighbor, fostering brushfire wars all over the world to keep everyone except the Soviet Union off-balance. Chaos was the stepping-stone to revolution.

Only this time it might backfire, and KGB Major General Mock knew it.

Carter spoke. "You mean that Moscow has ordered you to let them go?"

The Russian nodded. "Basically, yes. That is also why my hands are tied, to a degree." He inhaled deeply and his eyes bored intently into Carter's. "But I can help *you*. I can give you the intelligence that I have. Hopefully, it will lead you to the core of leaders. When that time comes, I may be able to help further, with men and arms, to wipe them out." He poured more brandy.

Carter took a moment to let this remarkable turn of events digest. "And if Moscow catches on?" he asked finally.

"Then," Mock said, raising his glass, a slight smile playing across his lips, "perhaps you could find me a little house in the wilds of Arizona."

•　　•　　•

For the next hour Carter took a history lesson, poring over documents and research reports as Mock set them on the desk before him.

Ala-Din Muhammed first gained recognition in October of 1092, when he ordered the assassination of the then Grand Vizier of Persia under the Turkish sultan Malik Shah, Nizam Al-Mulk.

Al-Mulk, surrounded by countless guards, was being carried back to his caravan from an audience with the people in a small village. Along the way, a half-naked holy man approaced the litter. He asked permission to kiss the vizier's ring as a token of respect. The guards granted the holy man his wish.

As he kissed the vizier's ring, the old man withdrew a dagger and slit the vizier's throat.

The holy man was immediately slashed to pieces, but within the hour all the surrounding countryside knew who was responsible for the killing.

Ala-Din Muhammed was a wildly religious fanatic, also known as "the wild man of the mountain." Through banditry and political assassination, he had amassed a fortune that allowed him to hire a vast army and build himself a practically impregnable fortress in the mountains of Persia.

He didn't stop with Al-Mulk's murder. He claimed the title of Grand Vizier for himself, and proceeded to assassinate all the tribal leaders around him. He claimed that he would usurp the Turks and return the country to the people.

To do this, he surrounded himself with a select group from the Ismaili sect and trained them as his personal assassins. Under the effects of wine laced with hashish, he convinced these men that they were superbeings and he was God incarnate.

He dubbed them The Order of the One Hundred Eyes, and so convinced them of his power that they willingly carried out suicide missions.

To prove this ultimate power of life and death to

guests and foreign dignitaries, he would order one of his followers to jump from a high window of the fortress to his death.

All who were ordered, obeyed.

Carter looked up from the manuscript. "Sounds like Khomeini."

"There are a lot of similarities," Mock agreed. "I think our modern-day Ala-Din Muhammed is following the master plan of the eleventh-century original, right down to the fortress."

"Any idea where it might be located?"

"Perhaps." Mock spread a map on the desk between them and used a pencil as a pointer. "There are two major uranium mines in Niger. Both of them are located in the mountainous Aïr region, approximately here, and here. About a year ago, two large shipments of raw uranium ore were stolen from the northernmost mine, here."

"I remember it," Carter said.

"The trucks headed for Algeria on this route, but they disappeared before they reached the frontier. I think they turned off, up into the mountains."

"You think there is a connection with this maniac?"

"Three months ago, I sent a three-man team into those mountains," Mock replied. "It was a solid cover, cleared through Niamey, the capital. They went in as independent, neutral geologists. They never came back."

"No trace?"

"None, and that area is like a mountainous replica of your Death Valley. Not even the nomads go in there."

Carter plucked a magnifying glass from the corner of the desk and studied the map closely. "Could we get a flyover?"

"I've done that, too . . . out of my pocket, by the way. Nothing. At least nothing you can see from the air. But that's not surprising. The Aïr Mountains are riddled with deep gorges and even high plateaus hidden by surrounding peaks."

Carter stood and stretched. "If he's in there, it would be like finding the proverbial needle in a haystack."

"There might be another way."

The tone in the old KGB agent's voice had radically altered, swiveling Carter's head instantly. "I'm listening."

"Those propaganda pamphlets had definite destinations." Again he used the pencil. "Accra in Ghana, Windhoek in Namibia, Mbabane in Swaziland, Addis Ababa in Ethiopia, and Berbera in Somalia."

Carter lit a cigarette and shook his head to clear it. "Cells?" he asked.

Mock nodded. "I think so. He's taken a page right out of the Soviet book for expansion. He's formed cells in all these areas, and probably several others, to sow unrest and to recruit."

It made sense, Carter thought; each of the areas mentioned already held thousands of displaced Africans in refugee camps, or were seats of constant upheaval.

"What are you suggesting?"

"I have pinpointed their cell in Berbera in Somalia. It is an office building on the Avenue d'Mer, near the main harbor."

"You're sure?" Carter said.

Mock patted his belly and leaned forward, self-satisfaction on his face. "The three terrorists who traded your two State Department officials for their freedom and a plane flew from Oman across the Gulf of Aden. The pilot was instructed to fly directly to Djibouti and land. He did, but when he landed at Djibouti, the three terrorists were not on board."

"They bailed out?"

Mock nodded. "They were picked up by a fishing boat and taken ashore at Berbera. My people trailed them to the building on the Avenue d'Mer."

"I think I see what you're driving at," Carter growled. "Dominoes."

"Exactly. Whoever this maniac is in his mountain

stronghold, his power lies in these cells and his communications with them."

"And if we knock over the Berbera cell, we might be able to pinpoint the others from the intelligence we find there." Carter sighed. "It's a long shot."

Mock's wide shoulders heaved and his arms raised in a "so what?" gesture. "At this time, without knowing the real identity of Ala-Din Muhammed, destroying his net and drawing him out is our only real chance."

It was Carter's turn to pace. "We'll need a neutral team, mercenaries. I can't go through Washington. They would never buy it."

Mock chuckled. "Nor would Moscow."

"We'll need funds."

"Once we find out Ala-Din's real identity, we'll use his. And, remember, he did not steal that uranium ore on a whim. There is a slim chance that he has the expertise to make a bomb . . . but there is that chance."

The Killmaster knew he didn't have much of a choice. He also guessed that David Hawk would go along with the wipeout as long as it couldn't be traced back to the U.S.

And then he remembered the key in his pocket. He fished the ring and the key out and showed it to Mock, explaining the significance Noreen Parris had placed on it.

"It would stand to reason," the Russian replied. "If the cluster of eyes in the ring is a cipher key . . ."

"And the One Hundred Eyes had to have some means of constant communication . . ."

Mock slapped the desk. "Then, whatever that key unlocks probably holds Nanwandu's master code book!"

"Noreen Parris," Carter said. "She knows where the key goes."

Mock jabbed a console on the desk. Instantly, the hatch opened and an aide stepped quickly into the room.

"Sir?"

"Radio Bahrain. I want to know where the Parris woman went when she was released!"

"*Da*, Comrade General."

It was an agonizing ten-minute wait until the aide returned.

"She continued on to the airport, Comrade General, and boarded a plane for Cyprus."

"Shit," Carter growled.

"I'm sorry," Mock said, "but I didn't dare bring an international journalist aboard the *Smoldosk*. Besides, I thought the woman had served her purpose."

"No matter," the Killmaster said with a shrug. "Do you have anyone on Cyprus?"

Mock chuckled. "Need you ask? Between your CIA and my people, we populate a large part of the island. I'll have her under surveillance the moment she lands."

"And," Carter added, "can you get me back ashore?"

Mock turned a lifted eyebrow to the aide.

"We cannot put you ashore in Manama, Bahrain, in broad daylight. The closest port would be Doha, in Qatar."

"How soon?" Carter asked.

"Six hours, at top speed," the aide replied.

"Change course," Mock growled, and the aide stepped briskly from the cabin. "Do you wish me to put the assault team together?"

Carter shook his head. "No, thanks. When the time comes to put my neck on the line, I want to know who's at my back."

"My dear Carter, after all I've told you, you still don't trust me?"

"Only up to the starting line, my dear General."

EIGHT

It was a grindingly slow, nail-biting process waiting for the *Smoldosk* to reach Qatar. Carter used the time to get himself whole again.

Thankfully, Mock's goons had taken his bag from the Mercedes and brought it aboard. That gave him a clean set of clothes and his tools—Wilhelmina, his 9mm Luger, and Hugo, his stiletto.

Customs in Qatar proved a little sticky. It wasn't often an American with a diplomatic passport disembarked from a Soviet fishing trawler. A shaky explanation that he was pursuing a new kind of détente did little good. A call to the British legation finally sprung him, and Carter made a beeline to the airport.

Once there, he had to use his VIP status to get a seat on a flight to Athens. From there it was no trouble obtaining a seat on Cyprus Airways on into Larnaca.

He had an hour before flight time, and used it to call home.

The AXE offices on Dupont Circle in Washington were humming.

Hawk had already had a meeting with the top dogs at State. It was about the way that Carter and Mock had figured. Fischer and Wright had diddled off on their own when Sir Martin Ramsey had slipped them the word of Hadj Bal-Sakiet's defection.

Their reprimand had been stiff, to the point where they both probably figured that they would have fared better being shot by the terrorists. As it was, they wouldn't be fired, but both of them would find themselves posted to the equivalent of Outer Mongolia.

Sir Martin Ramsey himself had been blatantly remiss in not informing MI6 of his pending coup. But because of his wife's death, the Brits were going easy on him for the time being.

The two dead terrorists in Oman had been tentatively identified. The man was Adee Molnai, the woman Oranomi Dileebu. Both were originally from Uganda, and members of the small Vezzine tribe. Though the tribe was poor, they had both been sent abroad in their youth to study in France. Little was known about either of them after leaving France, and Interpol had nothing of a criminal nature about either of them in their computers.

An interesting twist was the fact that Jabar Nanwandu was also a member of the Vezzine tribe.

Things were narrowing down. There wasn't a hell of a lot of cooperation with the current Ugandan government, but agents in place were trying to put the pieces together.

Carter gave a fast verbal report of everything he had gleaned from Noreen Parris, Maury Richland, and General Mock, which was all taped at the Washington end.

When this was done, the Killmaster requested that the tape be stopped, and he continued "ears only" for the chief of AXE, David Hawk.

The idea that General Mock wanted half the show with less than half of the actual participation didn't sit too well with the head of AXE. Carter succeeded in convincing him only when he reminded his chief that once before Mock had played square, in the Togo affair.

Also, it was common knowledge that the KGB had many more agents in place in the target areas than either AXE or the CIA. Intelligence—and its evaluation—would be far more available if Mock were in.

Hawk agreed at last, with the stipulation that the final intelligence spoils come to Washington.

Carter agreed, even when he knew that if he uncovered proof that the Soviets had used the One Hundred Eyes, he would probably have to face off Mock to keep it.

The two men signed off, with Carter detailing his immediate itinerary and Hawk assuring his agent that they would do everything possible to put the Ugandan pieces of the puzzle together.

Carter hung up and headed for his plane.

Mock's man in Cyprus was Yuri Pinskiy. The breadth of his shoulders strained a shabby raincoat, and his square, muscular face looked hewn from rough wood. His eyes were oddly soft. They were large brown cow's eyes with thick feminine lashes. But when he spoke, Carter knew the softness in his eyes was a deception.

"I think this form of cooperation between us is asinine, stupid, and dangerous," the big man stated bluntly as they stood at the baggage claim area. "However, I have my orders. And I will abide by them."

"Good of you," Carter said, and plucked his bag from the conveyer. "Shall we go?"

"The car is this way."

The car was an ancient American Chevrolet with more dents than a computer could compute and stuffing coming out of the seats. So much for the KGB budget on Cyprus.

There was a driver, a clone of Pinskiy, who neither spoke nor turned his head as they got into the car.

By time they had passed out of the airport proper

and gained the highway to Nicosia, Comrade Pinskiy
had taken a small vinyl-covered notebook from his
pocket.

"The woman was spotted in Athens at the airport.
She checked in for the Cyprus Airways flight, received a
boarding pass, checked her bag, and left the airport."

"What?"

"According to our man in Athens, she did not detect
him following her, but made foolish, amateurish at-
tempts to elude a tail."

"Your man stayed on her?"

"Of course. She went to the docks and booked pas-
sage on a cruise ship to Cyprus."

Carter shook his head. Noreen Parris was still playing
the spy. "You picked her up here?"

"Of course. She taxied to the local offices of one of
your wire services. There she filed a story. We have an
informer there. Here is a copy."

He produced a single sheet of paper and passed it to
Carter. The Killmaster scanned it once and then read it
again, slowly, word for word.

"Oh, Christ."

It was under her byline, a gossipy piece with lots of
"this reporter learned," and "according to a reliable
source" inferences. The gist of it was that a powerful
terrorist group had been formed in Africa. This group
had no known affiliation, but had been responsible for
several assassinations and kidnappings purely for profit
around the world.

Carter cursed her stupidity. She had named victims'
names, and promised that soon, "this reporter would
uncover the entire story."

The crowning glory was the last few sentences, when
she actually named the One Hundred Eyes.

"Get me to this wire service office as soon as possible," Carter growled.

Pinskiy spoke in rapid Russian to the driver and got a

grunt in return. But the car lurched ahead at a faster speed.

"Where is she now?"

Pinskiy flipped to another page of his notebook. "From the offices of the wire services, she went to Djebushi Street. There she spent a half hour in a watchmaker's shop. She must have made a telephone call there, because when she came out she was picked up by a limousine."

"A *what*?"

"Mercedes, chauffeured. License number FZ991-4. The Mercedes delivered her to the Oragon Hotel, where it dropped her off and she checked in. As of two hours ago, she was still in the hotel."

Carter dropped his head into his hands and furiously rubbed his temples with his fingertips in concentration.

Parris obviously thought that he, Carter, had been nabbed for good.

She had come to Cyprus to go after, all by herself, whatever the key in Carter's pocket would bring. Somehow she must have figured that she could get it without the key.

"Pinskiy . . ."

"*Da?*"

"Are you sure she called for the limousine from inside the watchmaker's shop?"

The Russian thought for a moment. "Not positive, no. It would have been imprudent to follow her inside at that point."

"Did your people make any note of her making a call from the Athens airport, or the docks before she boarded?"

Pinskiy flipped pages and nodded. "Yes. She made two, one from the airport and one from the docks."

Carter smiled. "And I'll bet you that when she got out of the limo to enter the hotel she had baggage."

Pinskiy's face blanched a shade or two and he glanced

forward at the driver. "Gregor?" he said, relaying Carter's question in Russian.

"*Da*, comrade," the man replied, and described the bag.

"He says—"

"Never mind, comrade," Carter growled. "I speak Russian."

The AXE man leaned back in the seat and closed his eyes as he lit a cigarette. Noreen Parris had some kind of a contact in Cyprus, and obviously one with money. That would explain the initial meet with Nanwandu and her access to a limo. He could pretty well guess the scenario for the next few hours, but he decided to play it out as it went, without trying to jump in all the way and risk the chance of picking up a Go Directly to Jail card.

Five minutes later they pulled up to a four-story whitewashed building that had turned a dismal gray over the years.

"The wire service is on the fourth floor, right," Pinskiy said without looking at Carter.

The Killmaster fished the key from his pocket and passed it to the other man. "Unless I miss my guess, that watchmaker also makes keys. Check this out and see if he made the woman one like it."

The Russian nodded.

"What was the name of the hotel?"

"Oragon."

"Yeah," Carter said, "meet me back there. I'll cab it when I'm done here."

The Russian took the key, still with his eyes straight ahead, as Carter stepped from the car and leaned back through the window.

"And, Pinskiy, if you have to bend his arm a little, do it. I'm sure Gregor there is good at that."

Without waiting for a reply, Carter turned and strolled into the building.

• • •

Carter knew the layout the moment he stepped into
the outer office. It was probably a two-man operation,
with a secretary who doubled on the machines. From
the sound, the machine room was behind a door to his
left. The chief of station and his reporter probably occupied a couple of desks behind the door to his right.

When Carter entered, the secretary was moving between an ancient, scarred desk and a worse-for-wear file
cabinet. She was a tall, statuesque brunette, about nine-
teen or twenty, with long flowing black hair, dark eye
makeup, and lots of lipstick. Under her denim jacket
was a soft cotton T-shirt. It read, in English, "I'd rather
be at the beach" and outlined rich, full nipples when the
jacket fell away.

"May I help you?"

"Depends. Who's your chief of station?"

"Mr. Travanti . . ."

"In there?"

"Yes. Who shall I say . . ." Carter was already past
her and at the door. "Wait, you can't—"

But Carter was already through the door and into the
office. It was as sparse and spare as the outer office,
with two desks, three chairs, a couple of filing cabinets,
and peeling paint.

One of the desks was occupied by a rather small, frail
man in his early thirties. He had a choirboy face that
looked barely mature enough to shave, and eyes that
darted from side to side like those of a hunted animal as
Carter approached him.

"See here . . ."

"I'm sorry, Mr. Travanti, I couldn't stop him . . ."
the secretary stammered.

"What's the meaning of this?" He looked Italian
—and probably was—but the English was Cambridge.

He was coming out of his chair as irately as he was

able, when Carter plopped his diplomatic passport on
the desk in front of him and sided it with his special ID.
The ID had SPECIAL AGENT in large block letters across
the top, with an explanation of same in ultrafine print
below it. His eyes went right to the presidential seal in
the lower right-hand corner, and he eased back into his
seat.

"That's quite all right, Miss Senta. You may leave us
alone."

Miss Senta's eyes got very wide under a suddenly furrowed brow, but she backed from the room and closed
the door behind her. Carter eased his left cheek onto the
desk and lit a cigarette.

"What have we done now?" Travanti asked, cough-
ing quietly as if something were suddenly caught in his
throat.

Carter filed that away for future leverage, and
dropped the copy of Noreen Parris's story on the desk.

"Jesus, where did you get this?"

"A little bird. I want it killed."

"Impossible. It went out hours ago." His eyes briefly
touched Carter's, then fluttered to the window as if that
were a means of escape.

The Killmaster took a flyer. "How many follow-
ups?"

"None."

"You're lying."

"Look, mister, there's such a thing as freedom of the
press—"

Carter put one finger on each side of the man's wind-
pipe and swiveled his head around until their eyes met.
"Look, Travanti, this is hotter than I want to mention.
You're right, I can't legally stop you. But I can advise."

The throat under Carter's fingers was jiggling like hell
in an attempt to swallow. "H-How so?"

"I can put the word on the street that you have the
follow-ups to the Parris story. I figure you'll get a caller

within the hour who'll be a helluva lot nastier than I am.''

It was bullshit, of course, but the guy bought it. With a shaky hand he pulled open the desk's center drawer and withdrew a manila envelope.

Carter scanned it, and cursed in four languages. "Believe me, pal, these stories would have set off a hornet's nest that nobody could have put a lid on.''

Travanti faded a few shades and choked. "You mean, uh, all that's true?''

"Yup. A lot of veiled innuendo, but enough is true to get somebody killed.''

Carter burned both stories in an empty wastebasket and sat down at the empty desk. For the next fifteen minutes, he hunted and pecked out a follow-up to the first story that considerably softened its clout.

Travanti shook even more when he read it. "Jesus, I can't send this . . .''

"Why not?''

"It's under Noreen Parris's byline. I can't do that!''

Carter picked up the phone and dialed direct. The call went through instantly. Carter explained the situation in quick, terse sentences, then handed the receiver to Travanti.

He took the phone as if it would bite him, and, in answer to a query from the other end, identified himself. From there on it was mostly, "Yes,'' "Yes sir,'' and "I understand sir,'' along with an increased amount of trembling in the frail body.

Carter knew why. The man on the other end was the State Department liaison between the president and David Hawk. His position had one hell of a lot of clout, and he was using it now on Travanti.

At last the little station chief bid a not-so-fond farewell and hung up the phone. A handkerchief appeared from a rear pocket and he mopped the sweat from his face and neck.

"Got it?" Carter asked.

"Got it," Travanti replied. "I'll put this on the wire right away."

"Appreciate it," Carter chuckled, and headed for the door.

"If you see Parris, tell her from now on to send her stuff direct. I don't want to see her again."

"I'll do that. And, by the way . . ."

"Yes?"

"Who passes your stuff to the KGB? Your stringer, or Miss Senta?"

"The girl," Travanti replied with a sick smile. "I ignore it. What the hell, on my budget I can't pay her half what she's worth. I figure the Russians would get it anyway, why not make them pay? Hey, wait a minute . . ."

Carter could see the light bulbs go on in the Italian's mind.

"His name is Pinskiy," Carter said. "Not my type, really, but the fact that we're cooperating will show you just how big this thing is."

He walked by Miss Senta with a wink and headed downstairs to find a cab.

The Oragon was Old World and somewhat the worse for wear, but it had a lot of charm. It also had a cozy lounge just off the lobby, where Pinskiy and his clone sat sipping two domestic beers.

Carter smiled. Once again, the KGB budget for foreign agents reared its head.

The Killmaster ordered expensive imported Russian vodka and enjoyed their reaction.

"Well?" he asked as soon as the waiter had retreated.

"She only stayed in the hotel about a half hour, and then checked out."

"That figures," Carter grunted. "The limousine?"

Pinskiy nodded. "I had two men here on her. One

followed the Mercedes. The other is waiting at a contact point for word.''

"What about the key?"

Pinskiy produced it and passed it to Carter. "There's a code, here, on the edge. You can barely see it with the naked eye."

"What does it match?"

"Hotel safe-deposit box."

Carter groaned again. He didn't want to ask, but he did. "What hotel?"

"This one, the Oragon."

Carter remembered the tiny glass that Noreen Parris had used to magnify her eyes to apply makeup. It had been on the vanity when they had examined the ring and the key.

That's when she had copied the code.

"She had another key made, and checked in just long enough to use it."

Pinskiy shrugged. "So it would appear."

Carter stood, taking a thick wad of paper napkins from the table and shoving them into his pocket. "Where's my bag?"

"At the desk," the clone said in fair English.

"Come up to my room and let me know where the woman went as soon as you know."

The Killmaster stopped at the bar.

"Yes, sir?"

"Send a bottle of good Russian vodka to my friends over there." He dropped an American bill on the bar. "And keep the change."

"Yes, sir!"

In the lobby, he stopped at the stationery desk. The paper napkins went into an envelope, which he sealed, then he continued on to the front desk.

There were two people on duty—a gray-haired concierge who looked as if he'd arrived with the hotel's original bricks, and a young, gum-chewing assistant.

Carter timed his approach so the assistant was busy with a guest.

"Good evening, sir," the old man said.

"My bag was left here at the desk. Fields is the name. I'll need a room."

He registered, passed over his Fields passport, and requested a safe-deposit box. The concierge disappeared behind a partition, motioning Carter to follow.

There were about fifty boxes. Most of them sported keys. The concierge chose one and opened it with his master key.

"Just close the box and withdraw the key when you are finished, sir. It will lock automatically."

Carter already had the napkin-stuffed envelope in his hand. "Thank you."

Moments later, Carter was back in the lobby following an ancient bellman into the elevator.

In the room he stripped down, shaved, and showered. He dressed in a pair of lightweight slacks and a pullover shirt. Over this he added a sweater, and, noticing that the drizzle outside had turned to rain, shook out a raincoat from the bag.

Twenty minutes later there was a knock on the door and Pinskiy entered. Wordlessly he crossed to the bed and spread out a map of the island.

"Please don't tell me," Carter said, "that she went over to the Turkish side."

Since the 1974 invasion by Turkey, the island of Cyprus had been divided: Turkish military controlled the north and Greece controlled the south. Even the capital city of Nicosia, like Berlin, had been partitioned.

Operating in any way in the north under the Turkish military was nearly impossible.

"We are lucky," Pinskiy replied. "The woman was taken here, about three kilometers west of Paphos.

There is a new road from Nicosia to Limassol. Once there, we can drive west along the coast to Paphos."

"No, it will be better for both of us if she doesn't know your people are involved. I'll rent a car and go alone."

The Russian shrugged and folded the map. "Suit yourself."

"What's the situation?"

"The estate is owned by Constantin Damos."

"The newspaper tycoon?"

"The very same. Madame Maria Damos is a Greek-American, born in New York. She is a quite famous writer and reporter in her own right."

Carter nodded. "That's probably the connection with Noreen Parris. Get me a car. I'll meet you outside in fifteen minutes."

The Russian handed Carter the map and lumbered toward the door.

"And, Pinskiy . . ."

"*Da*?"

"A *new* car."

The KGB man grimaced and left, leaving the door open behind him.

The Killmaster shrugged into Wilhelmina's shoulder rig, checked the Luger's clip, and holstered it. Then he rolled up his right sleeve and attached the stiletto's chamois sheath to his right forearm. Before rolling the sleeve down and donning his coat, he tensed his forearm to test the spring. The stiletto shot forward, the hilt settling firmly into his palm.

Carter doubted that he would need his tools in the next few hours, but he didn't feel completely dressed without them.

When his bag was packed, he took the creaking elevator down to the lobby. Near the desk he dawdled until the old concierge was occupied, and then approached the younger assistant.

"A last-minute change of plans. I'm afraid I'll have to check out."

"Your key, please, sir?"

Carter gave it to him and waited, fingering Nan-wandu's safe-deposit box key in his palm. When the bill was totaled, he paid it and flashed the key.

"I also have a box."

The clerk checked it and nodded. "This way, sir."

Carter followed him around the partition, sure that, hours before, Noreen Parris had used the same subter-fuge and the box would be empty.

"Your key, sir?"

Carter passed it over. The man inserted it and his master key. When it was unlocked, he pulled it out an inch or two and turned to Carter.

"Just leave your key in the box, sir."

"I'll do that."

When he was alone, he flipped the lid up.

He was wrong. The box wasn't empty. Inside was a single, folded slip of paper. He opened it and read with disgust: *Carter: I don't know what happened to you, but if you get this far, this is to let you know that I found the box empty. I'm catching the next plane to London, and then on to New York. I've decided there's no story after all. Parris.*

"Bullshit," Carter hissed, and pocketed the note.

If he had harbored one tiny shred of illusion about the integrity of Noreen Parris, he had now lost it.

He slammed the box back into its slot and searched for the box that he had rented when he checked in. When he found it, he left the key and headed back into the lobby.

The younger concierge looked up as the Killmaster passed. "Everything all right, sir?"

"No. Lousy."

Pinskiy and his driver had parked about a block from

the hotel. The car was an Italian Fiat, fairly new and without dents.

Carter nodded his approval when Pinskiy handed him the keys. "Yours?"

"Rented. You can drop it off at Lanarca or back here."

"Good enough. Get out your notebook. Get in touch with Mock, and have him put his radios and computers to work. I need an expatriate American named Rowland. James Rowland. He runs a high-stakes floating poker game off a yacht called the *Long Shot* in the Med. Mock found him for me once before; he can probably do it again. Got it?"

Pinskiy nodded.

"Also, another expatriate Yank named Hardy. He goes by the name of Ace, but Alphonso is on his passport. I think he was named after Al Capone. Last time I heard, he was in Marseille. Last on the list is Colonel Trig Muldune. He's a merc now, was in the SAS. He's British, and if he's not in jail in England he could be anywhere. That's it."

Pinskiy flipped the notebook shut and let a sour grimace fill his face.

"Something wrong?" Carter asked.

"I think I know your Mr. Trig Muldune."

Carter smiled and crawled into the Fiat. "I figured you would. He's the same Colonel Muldune who whipped the shit out of your Cuban friends down in Angola." The engine purred to life. "Meet me at Lanarca Airport."

"When?" Pinskiy asked.

Carter chuckled. "When I get there."

The little car bolted forward and Carter fished a cigarette from his breast pocket.

There was indeed, he thought, a certain satanic satisfaction in working with the KGB. He could needle the hell out of them.

NINE

In the aftermath of the Greco-Turkish troubles in Cyprus, it was the Greeks who had the last laugh. They got the southern end of the island—the most beautiful part—after division. And the village of Paphos, even near midnight, was a garden spot.

Carter drove slowly through the village and regained the coast road. Under a crystal-clear sky, moonlight made the sea glow to his left, and Carter mused.

He was passing very near the spot where Aphrodite, the Greek goddess of desire, was supposed to have risen naked and fully formed from the sea.

Right now, Carter thought, *I could use the lift of spirits a naked Aphrodite could give!*

And then the corners of his mouth turned down and the taste of his cigarette grew stale. There would be no Aphrodite this night. Only Noreen Parris.

The Villa Damos stood alone on a rocky promontory directly above the sea. The inland borders of the grounds were enclosed by a high stone fence, but there was no gate, only two large statues on each side of a narrow drive.

The villa itself was set back on a vast expanse of

property, and it looked more like a casino than a private residence. It sported a lot of black marble—some real, some ersatz—several Greek columns, incongruous, ugly cupolas, and wide terraces. About a third of the downstairs rooms were ablaze with light.

The long, curving drive led up to a shiny black façade where bronze doors were hung between two fat white columns. The Mercedes stretch limousine was parked in the center of the drive. Carter parked behind it and mounted the twenty or so steps to the door.

"Yes?"

The butler was English, and looked a bit like Abe Lincoln without a beard. His facial expression reminded Carter of an undertaker who had just learned his best friend had been cremated by a rival establishment while still owing him three hundred dollars.

"Carter. Nick Carter."

"Yes?"

The Killmaster passed over his card. "Amalgamated Press and Wire Services. I'm to meet Constantin Damos here."

The frown on the butler's face was his first sign of life. "I don't understand. Mr. Damos has not returned from Athens—"

Carter jumped in. "Yeah, I know. He told me to come ahead. I'm sure if I could talk to Mrs. Damos . . ."

By this time Carter was past him and into the hall.

"I'll take your card to Mrs. Damos and ask if she will see you."

"You do that."

The butler led him across marble floors, through a vast reception room dominated by a double curving staircase, to a comparatively small sitting room where everything was pastel and gilt and fragile and expensive.

"A drink, sir?" he said, motioning Carter to a sideboard.

"Yeah, I'll help myself. You get the missus."

"Very well, sir," he replied stiffly, glancing again at the card. "American?"

"Yeah," Carter replied, showing a lot of teeth. "How'd you know?"

"I just guessed," he replied dryly, and left the room.

Carter built himself a whiskey and studied some fat angels who hung heavily from a too-blue ceiling.

The house was so still, Carter could hear a clock ticking in the hall. It made him conscious of time, and he looked at his watch. It was almost midnight.

Had La Parris filed another story by phone on her find? He hadn't contacted Pinskiy's watcher, who was somewhere out there in the darkness. Maybe he should have. Maybe Parris had already flown.

The room suddenly depressed him. He freshened his drink and moved to a pair of French doors that opened at a touch. Beyond them was a narrow terrace. He had barely stepped outside when, in the distance, somewhere near the road, he heard the sound of a car starting.

The sound of a door opening and closing brought him back into the room.

A woman stood by the sideboard. She was slim, and dressed in a neck-to-floor scarlet robe, and even in the dim light Carter could see that she was a woman who would never lack male attention.

Her dark hair was cut extremely short in a boyish fashion, but any resemblance to the male sex ended there. There was a starkness in the face that robbed it of exceptional beauty but gave her a haunting quality that riveted Carter's attention.

"You are Mr. Carter . . .?" she asked, checking the card in her hand.

"That's right," he replied, crossing the room until he was standing directly in front of her.

Fantastic dark eyes came up to meet his. "I'm sorry, but my husband never contacted me about your arrival."

"That's probably because I never talked to your husband, Mrs. Damos."

The eyes got very cold. "Then I'm afraid you'll have to leave."

"Not until I've seen Noreen Parris."

"I don't know anyone by that name."

She reached for a bell cord at her shoulder, and Carter's hand came out like a snake to grasp her wrist.

"I wouldn't call your butler unless you want him to get hurt."

"See here, Mr. Carter—"

"No, Mrs. Damos, *you* see here. I know Noreen Parris is here. I know she has something I want, and I'm going to get it."

She crumbled a little and leaned against the wall. Carter released her and got rid of his glass.

"Are you one of the men trying to kill her?" She spoke as if she were fighting panic.

Carter only shook his head. It was obvious that Noreen Parris was willing to use—and misuse—old friends as much as she used old agents.

"Look, Mrs. Damos, I don't know what kind of cock-and-bull story she told you, but if I'm anything, I'm one of the guys trying to keep her alive."

She looked nervously over her shoulder and seemed reassured to find no one there. "Noreen and I are very dear friends. How do I know you don't mean to harm her?"

She didn't even see the hand move; suddenly Carter's Luger was in front of her face. At the same time, he brought one of her hands up and curved the fingers around the butt. There was a sharp click and her eyes grew wide as he jacked a shell into the chamber.

"The safety is here. There's a shell ready to fire. All you have to do is point it and pull the trigger."

"M-me?"

"Yeah. If I start to hurt her, you can shoot me."

"My God, put that thing away!" she gasped, sliding past Carter and pouring herself a drink. "I hate guns."

"Me, too," Carter said. "But they're convincing in more ways than one."

"She's upstairs sleeping. She was dog tired when she got here. Said all she wanted to do for the next ten hours was sleep. She didn't even eat dinner."

"I'm a little short of time . . ."

Again the eyes, this time calm. "You look like a killer, but suddenly you don't seem dangerous to me. Isn't that odd?"

"I grow on you. Shall we go?"

He followed her out into the vast reception hall. Her heels made little clicking sonds on the marble as they climbed the stairs. It was warm and humid outside, but in here a cold draft seemed to be sweeping down from the upper halls. On the second floor, she led the way down a wide hall strewn with statuary to a double door at the end.

She pushed open the doors and they stepped into a large, ornately furnished sitting room. On either side of the sitting room, doors opened into bedrooms. With a nod of her head she indicated the bedroom on the right. The door was open. Carter could see an enormous bed complete with a satin spread already turned down for the night.

"That's my bedroom."

The way she said it had a lot of meaning. Carter chose to ignore it. "And Noreen?"

"This is the guest room."

She veered to the left and Carter followed. There was no answer to the first or second knock.

"Noreen? Noreen, it's Maria."

Still no answer.

"That's odd, she's usually a light sleeper."

She tried the door. It was locked, or so Carter thought. Frantically, she turned the knob and pushed the door open about an inch.

"What is it?" Carter asked.

"There's something holding it, something lodged under the knob on the other side. The lock is broken . . ."

Carter pushed her aside and threw his weight against the door. Fortunately, whatever was blocking it from the other side was fragile. He could feel it giving.

On the third try there was the sound of splintering wood and the door burst inward on darkness. Carter checked his forward movement when his feet collided with the remnants of a chair. At the same time, he shoved Maria Damos back into the sitting room.

"Stay out there!" he hissed, and dropped to one knee with his back against the wall and his right hand full of Wilhelmina.

Across the darkness he could make out draperies fluttering against an open, moonlit window. Beyond, he saw the delicate ironwork of a balcony railing outlined against the night sky.

From somewhere in the room he could hear muffled breathing. He felt above him along the wall for a light switch, his free hand clutching the Luger.

At last he found it, and suddenly the room was flooded with light. The scene it revealed was so bizarre that all Carter could do was crouch and stare.

Behind him, in the doorway, Maria Damos let go with a muffled scream. "Noreen!"

The room was in wild disorder. Chairs were overturned, drawers flung to the floor, clothes strewn about, and cushions slashed and mangled.

And on the bed, her arms stretched above her head and secured to the headboard, was Noreen Parris. Her legs were similarly bound to the footboard, and a pillowcase had been stuffed in her mouth and bound by a pair of pantyhose.

She was desperately writhing about; her eyes above

the gag were those of a crazed and trapped animal.

And she was as naked as the day she was born.

Carter managed to get to the bed before Maria Damos, and pulled off the gag.

It was barely off when Noreen screamed in white-hot fury, "The book! That son of a bitch took it!"

"Who was it?" Carter asked for the second time, idly toying with the pantyhose.

Noreen didn't look up at him. She only coughed for the second time, sitting on the edge of the bed. It was obvious to the Killmaster that she was trying to get her wits about her as she clutched a robe together around her with one hand and sipped brandy from a snifter in the other.

Maria Damos had fetched the robe and the brandy. Now she stood at the foot of the bed, smoking a cigarette and gazing at her old friend with a jaundiced eye. At least it looked jaundiced enough to Carter that he guessed the woman was more than halfway on his side.

"Shouldn't I call the police?" she asked.

"Mrs. Damos," Carter said, not taking his eyes from Noreen Parris, "let's just say I'm the police, okay?"

"But—"

"He's right, Maria, no police," Noreen said.

"I'll tell you what, Maria," Carter said, taking the woman's hand and guiding her to the door, "why don't you go get Abe Lincoln . . ."

"Abe Lincoln?"

"Your butler. Go get him moving and fix us some coffee. It's been a long night, and it's not over yet."

She chuckled. "There's nothing like coffee, a burglary, and a handsome man to keep one awake."

Maria Damos was no dummy. She recognized real authority when she saw it, as well as a born liar, namely Noreen. She also understood when she wasn't wanted.

She went quietly, and Carter closed the door behind

her. He turned and faced Noreen.

"Who was it?" he growled.

"You've made a conquest," the woman replied dryly, ignoring the question. "You should take advantage of it. Maria is a very beautiful woman."

"Who was it?" Carter repeated.

Silence.

"You called him a son of a bitch when I pulled the gag off. Who was it!"

"I haven't the faintest idea," she said in the tone of a person who has made a decision. "I had just showered. I came out of the bathroom and I was just over the threshold when I realized my bedroom lights were off. I stopped, but it was too late. Someone grabbed me. I tried to scream, but he tore away the towel I was carrying and wrapped it around my head. He was strong . . . I thought he was going to kill me. When he pushed me down on the bed, my head hit the headboard. I must have gone out for a moment. When I came to, my hands and feet were already bound and . . . the bastard!"

Carter didn't believe a word she was saying, but he accepted it for the time being. "Okay, what about the book?"

"What about it?"

Carter sighed and slammed the glass from her hand. It shattered against the far wall, and before the sound died out he had the pantyhose around her wrists, her arms above her head, and he was tying her to the headboard.

"What the hell are you doing?"

"Tying you up again."

"The hell you are! I'll—"

"Then I'm going to torture you."

"Go to hell."

"What about the book?" he hissed.

"Oh, for crissakes, get that smug expression off your face. All right, it was a code book. It was all made up of signs of the Zodiac, astrological equations, I don't know what else. I don't think it could be figured out without the ring."

"And I had the ring."

She shrugged. "I was going to get in touch with you."

"Sure you were."

"I was!"

Suddenly her body slumped and a lot of the fire went out of her eyes. She looked tired and haggard.

"Who got the book?"

"Maury Richland."

Carter rummaged until he found two more pair of pantyhose. With these he tied her kicking legs to the footboard.

"You bloody sod, I told you what you wanted to know!"

"Maybe. Don't worry, I'll be back."

Downstairs, Carter found a kitchen the size of most houses. Maria Damos was making the coffee herself.

"Whitney is frightened out of his wits. I told him to stay in bed."

"Noreen is resting," Carter said. "Let's not disturb her for a while."

There was a blood-curdling scream, followed by a long string of curses from the upper reaches of the house as Carter exited into the garden. Over his shoulder he could see Maria Damos calmly smoking a cigarette.

She hadn't heard a thing.

He moved through the gardens on a line from Noreen's bedroom window. From a couple of broken branches on a tree, he had already figured Richland's entrance and exit. An iron grillwork gate almost over-grown with greenery stood in the wall. There was no lock on it and it hung half open.

Carter went through and followed a path along the wall. It looked as if it ran all the way to the road, and then he remembered the car he had heard starting up while he stood on the terrace waiting for Maria Damos.

If the driver had been Maury Richland, that meant . . .

The Killmaster found Pinskiy's man about ten feet off the path. He was out cold and sitting with his back up against a tree.

There was a note rolled up and stuck down between his vest and shirt: *I spotted the bitch when she made the pickup at the Oragon, then followed this one following her. Since when are you footsie-footsie with the Volga boatmen? And why does Parris work alone again? I smell a double-cross. Stay by the phone.*

It wasn't hard to figure the synopsis of events. Richland followed Noreen from Behrain, and also picked up on her Russian tail. In Nicosia he hit on the watchmaker who also made keys, and he'd guessed the rest.

Carter checked the KGB man's pulse, figured Richland had used a hypo of some kind, and returned to the house. Maria Damos was still in the kitchen. Upstairs, Noreen Parris was still screaming.

"You're back."

"I'll be leaving soon," Carter said.

"Coffee?"

"Thank you." He accepted the cup and nodded toward the phone on the counter at her elbow. "When that rings, I'll answer it."

"And how soon after you leave do you want me to untie her?"

Carter grinned. "Mrs. Damos, it's a pity you're married."

She smiled. "My husband is a good deal older than I, and he's a very understanding man . . ."

"I think about two hours will give me enough time." The phone rang and Carter answered it. "Hello, Maury . . ."

TEN

Carter extinguished his cigarette and followed the flow of humanity into the Milan opera house. He waited five minutes in line before he reached one of the ticket windows.

"I believe a ticket has been left for me. Carter, Nicholas Carter."

"Si, signore." A small envelope slid through the cage. "It has been paid for, signore."

"Grazie."

He moved back into the milling crowd and checked the envelope. It was a private box. Maury Richland wasn't taking any chances.

It had been almost forty-eight precious hours since Carter had taken the call in Maria Damos's kitchen, and he could remember every word:

"Hello, Maury."

"You got the note."

"I did."

"Did you bring the Russkies in?"

"I did," Carter had replied. "You've got the book, I've got the key. Let's get together. Where are you?"

"Lanarca Airport, but I leave in ten minutes."

Cute, Carter had thought. Richland had timed the call so he couldn't be stopped. "How do we work it, Maury?"

"The opera, in Milan, day after tomorrow. A ticket will be waiting for you at the La Scala box office."

"Milan?"

"That's right. I've got the goods, and this time we meet on neutral ground. Bring the cash, all of it."

"You're sure you want it that way, Maury?"

"I'm sure. I just want out with my skin and some traveling money. Your Russkie friends have stirred up the One Hundred Eyes with all their questions. It's too hot for me."

"It's a deal, but I think you're stupid," Carter had sighed. "They know you made the connection with Nanwandu. You're probably on their list."

"That's why I'm disappearing. Oh, by the way, ever hear of a big bad black chap named Jacob Borassa?"

"Doesn't ring a bell."

"Well, have your Russian buddies or your hotshots in Washington check him out. Jacob Borassa is the pro who took Nanwandu and Collis out. Watch your tail, Nicky, lad. They may have a number on you, too."

The line had gone dead. Carter immediately redialed Lanarca and learned that a flight to Rome was in final boarding.

Maury Richland hadn't forgotten all the tricks of the trade, and Carter wasn't surprised that the man still had contacts who could—and would—feed him information.

Carter had indeed watched his tail for the next, very busy, forty-eight hours.

In Rome he had contacted Dupont Circle. Reluctantly, they had come up with the cash, but only after Carter had given them as much assurance as he could that the slush fund would be reimbursed when they found the funding source for the One Hundred Eyes.

He also passed on the name Richland had given him, Jacob Borassa, to feed into the computers.

Next he contacted General Mock. The KGB net had been busy. Ace Hardy had been located in Barcelona. He was running a strip joint called La Muñequita Papel. Rowland had also been located. He was in jail in the port of Cagliari on the island of Sardinia. It seems that he had gotten too close to the mayor's wife after already fleecing the mayor's brother.

This would, of course, pose a problem, but it could be overcome. It wouldn't be the first time Carter had sprung someone from a foreign jail for a bit of business.

As yet, former SAS Colonel Trig Muldune's whereabouts had not been located.

Carter had then brought Mock up to date on Maury Richland and the existence of the code book. Both men agreed that the book could be the means to crack everything open if there was a way into the cult's communications net.

Mock would have a top cryptanalyist awaiting Carter in Milan.

At noon that day, he had checked into the Francia Europa on the Corso Vittorio Emanuele, and now he was entering the huge and revered La Scala opera house.

The massive interior, with its semicircular rows of boxes and balconies, was almost as glittering as the stage. The box that Maury Richland had somehow commandeered was on the grand tier, second box from the stage on the left.

Carter passed his ticket badge to a tuxedoed watchdog, and was ushered into a little private sitting room to which one could retire when boredom with the opera itself set in.

A small table had been set up with hors d'oeuvres and iced champagne. Carter plucked a canapé from one of the trays and moved through a pair of velvet curtains into the box itself.

The house was full of beautiful people. Across the way and below were row upon row of white shirt fronts, formal gowns draped with summer furs, and the glitter of diamonds catching the warming lights from the stage.

But the box was empty. On the seat of each velvet chair was a program, reminding Carter that he didn't even know what opera he would probably be walking out on within the next hour.

It was Puccini's *Tosca*.

"Scusi, signore . . ."

Carter almost came out of his chair. He whirled, and barely arrested the movement of his hand toward the Luger stuck into his cummerbund and trousers in the small of his back.

Standing in a break in the curtains was a huge black man in a white waiter's jacket. He had come through the outer sitting room and up to the curtains as quietly as a cat.

"Yes?"

"Is everything all right, signore? More champagne, perhaps?"

His Italian, Carter noted, was flat, as a Frenchman would speak the language.

"No, no, everything is fine."

"If you wish anything, signore, just ring the bell, there. I will be serving your box this evening."

"Grazie."

The man faded as quietly as he had come. Carter moved to the curtain and watched him through a crack.

Nothing out of the ordinary. He checked the ice in the two champagne buckets, added a little, moved the platter of hors d'oeuvres around a little, and ambled into the hallway.

Carter sensed the houselights dimming, and turned to face the stage.

Where was Richland? What kind of a game was he playing?

Suddenly the curtain rose, and in muted light Carter saw the church of Saint'Andrea della Valle, and, just to the right of that, the chapel of the Attavanti family.

There was no overture to *Tosca*. The opera commenced with three striking chords, given out with the full power of the orchestra.

Carter heard the chords and saw the character of Angelotti enter.

"At last," the character sang. "In my foolish fright I took every face I saw for that of a police agent."

Tosca had begun, and there was no Maury Richland.

Carter had no choice. He checked the sitting room one more time, found it as empty as before, and took one of the plush chairs at the rear of the box in shadows.

It was just after the initial meeting of Angelotti and Cavaradossi when the curtains just behind the Killmaster's shoulder parted and one of the tuxedoed attendants slipped through. He carried a small silver tray in front of him. On it was a small brown envelope.

"You are Signore Carter?"

"Si."

"For you, signore."

Carter plucked the envelope from the tray and replaced it with a five-thousand-lira note. He dangled a second note of the same denomination above the first.

"Did you see the person who sent the note?"

"No, signore," the man replied, eyeing the bill with obvious regret. "It was sent to the box office . . . a messenger service."

Carter nodded and dropped the bill. The man smiled his gratitude and faded through the curtains, and Carter ripped open the envelope:

I told you to watch your tail, pally. You've got two of them right on you. Don't be surprised—they're good. But you brought them, now you lead them away so we can do business. Put the money under the front row aisle seat in the hat wire. Leave during the first interval. Come back and collect after the second. I don't care where you go, but make it far enough away so I can get in and out safely. I'll be watching. M.

Carter had no choice. He had to trust Richland that, once he collected, he would leave the book in place of the money.

He pocketed the note and unfastened the cummerbund around his waist. It was actually a money belt. It would look odd moving around without the cummerbund, but he could keep his jacket buttoned.

The voices of the chorus were just finishing the *"Te aeternum patrem omnis terra veneratur"* as Carter, in a crouch, waddled down the aisle. He rolled the cummerbund/money belt tightly and slipped it into the hat wire under the seat.

By the time he had returned to the rear of the box, the curtain was descending to thunderous applause. Carter didn't wait for it to die, but moved out through the small sitting room and into the long curving hallway behind the boxes.

It was still fairly empty, as were the grand staircase and the huge, ornate foyer. Less than two minutes later he was moving down the long tier of exterior stairs. Near the bottom, he paused to light a cigarette.

From behind the flame and his cupped hands he saw one of them: a taxi driver, lounging on the fender of his cab near the center of the piazza.

Carter turned left and moved along the line of limousines and their chauffeurs, who stood in little clusters, smoking and talking. As he walked, Carter donned a pair of what appeared to be common, tinted glasses.

As he unfolded them, he locked into place hidden hinges in the arms of the frames, arching them away from his head. When they were in place he glanced to the left, to the right, then straight ahead, and smiled in satisfaction.

The glasses allowed him a full 360-degree view. Each side's tapered, curved lens was actually two lenses fused together; straight ahead they were regular sunglasses, but when the arms were locked in the angled position, the sides of the lenses mirrored the area to the rear of the wearer.

In the improvised rearview mirrors, the Killmaster saw the cab move empty away from the stand and fall in behind him.

Three blocks from the opera house, the cab suddenly disappeared. But in its place was another one, the driver intent on Carter's back.

He was eight blocks from La Scala by now, and the pedestrian traffic was thickening. Carter slowed his pace. He didn't want to lose the tail.

On the next corner, two girls lounged in a way that said For Sale. A three-wheeled *gelati* wagon stopped in front of them. One of the girls bought an ice cream.

In the middle of the next block, Carter saw a neon sign saying Caffè Roma. As he veered toward the entrance, he saw the cab speed up and then slow at the corner. He couldn't see the signal, but one of the ice cream girls came tripping his way.

They were good, Carter thought, very good. No wonder he hadn't spotted them.

The wide terrace of the Caffè Roma was only thinly populated. He found a table near the rear and ordered a Campari and soda. It came just as the woman walked through the door and took a stool at the bar.

Maury Richland had been wrong. There were more than two of them, several more. Carter hoped the ex-MI6 man was watching close enough.

In the next half hour, he checked his watch every five minutes and did away with the two Camparis. As he paid his bill, the woman scooted out the front door.

Outside on the square, neither the taxi nor either one of the women were in sight.

Had they dropped the tail? And, if so, why?

Carter walked a slow, measured pace back to La Scala and found that the opera was now in the second interval. The smartly dressed audience had spilled out through the lobbies into the streets under a cloud of cigarette smoke and laughter.

Carter shouldered his way into the main foyer and climbed the grand staircase. Halfway up he paused, his eyes searching the crowd below.

Beautifully gowned women and their escorts were arranged in gay, chattering groups down the marble steps like extras in the grand finale of a lush Hollywood period musical.

Down below, on the floor of the main lobby, there were mobs around each of the champagne bars. Behind them, handsome young men in white jackets and black trousers with red stripes up the seams worked furiously. Other young men dressed the same way moved through the crowd with trays.

The three-minute warning bell signifying the end of the interval sounded faintly above the babble. No one paid any attention.

No one but Carter. One of the white-coated waiters moved up the stairs toward him.

Suddenly the Killmaster felt a chill of apprehension dart up his spine.

"Sciampagna, signore?"

"No, grazie."

The waiter moved on, with Carter's eyes glued to his trousers. He shut his eyes, saw the waiter who had entered the box, and opened them again.

There had been no red stripes on the black waiter's trousers.

Carter whirled. There must have been fifty waiters

milling around the main foyer and on the stairs. Not a single one of them was black.

Carter bolted up the stairs, shouldering his way through the crowd making its way back into the theater. Inside, he could hear the orchestra striking up the first chords of music.

The circular hall behind the boxes was less crowded, allowing the Killmaster to almost sprint. The music hit a crescendo and the lights dimmed as Carter reached the sitting room door.

It was slightly ajar.

He closed it behind him and drew Wilhelmina as he moved quickly to the curtains of the box. Parting them, he darted inside and came up short, as if his feet were suddenly caught in ice.

Maury Richland sat in the second aisle, slumped forward over the backs of the first-row seats.

Gently, Carter grasped his shoulder and pulled him back.

The piano wire garrote was embedded so deeply in Richland's throat that it couldn't be seen.

Obviously Maury, like Carter, had underestimated them. Whoever Jacob Borassa was, he was thorough. And deadly.

From the looks of it, Richland had had no inkling that his killer was right behind him.

Then Carter saw a red cummerbund on the seat beside the body. He straightened the dead man, and saw his own black cummerbund around Richland's waist.

Evidently the assassin had only one order: kill. There had been no order to search the body or, Carter was sure, that amount of cash would have been lifted.

That could mean . . .

Carter stopped and felt under the front-row aisle seat. His fingers found a small, oilskin package. Inside the pouch was a pocket-size notebook. One glance at a few pages told him he had found gold.

He pocketed the notebook and moved back to the corpse. "Sorry, old buddy."

When the black cummerbund was back around his own waist, he patted down the pockets and removed everything that would identify the body.

The hallway was empty. The waiters would be counting their tips and the ushers would be changing. Their night was done.

Trying to find Borassa—if the assassin had indeed been Borassa—would be impossible. He would be long gone.

Two blocks from La Scala, Carter dumped the contents of Maury Richland's pockets in a nearly full garbage can and hailed a taxi.

All the way to the hotel he checked for a tail.

There wasn't any.

Poor Maury, he thought, it was him they had tagged all along. But they hadn't known about the book.

And, with any luck, that would bury them.

ELEVEN

At the hotel, Carter paid the cabbie and entered the lobby. It was nearly midnight and the lounge was jumping. He moved through it without a pause, passed the men's room, and walked swiftly down a long hall toward the employees' entrance.

The alley behind the hotel was empty. Carter strolled briskly to a small side street, this time with every sense alert. It was obvious that Jacob Borassa and Company were as good or better than most. Carter didn't plan on being the man's next victim.

It was a fifteen-block walk to the Brera district, but he covered twice that in a zigzag pattern before he slipped through the door of a cellar joint called La Grotta del Viavolo.

The name "devil's cave" fit. Even the bored bartender looked a little like Satan in a white shirt and black bow tie. There were three equally bored hookers at the bar, a couple at a table staring longingly into each other's eyes, and a waitress.

Through the gloom, Carter saw his man in a smoky corner. He was a short, chunky man with a square, bulldog face that appeared to have reached middle age reluctantly and then dared time to push it further. A thin black cigar dropped from barely-there lips, and droopy eyes regarded Carter from behind heavy-lensed glasses.

He looked like an accountant, but according to Mock, Serge Shalinov was the best code man in Europe.

"Campari . . . there," Carter growled, passing the waitress.

At the table, he slid into a chair beside Shalinov so they could both observe the room. He noticed a pistol resting between the man's legs.

"I don't think you'll need that," Carter said, exchanging a bill for the Campari and shooing the waitress away.

"I'll be the judge of that," the man replied in a voice that sounded like gravel raining on a tin roof. "They found a man murdered at La Scala about an hour ago . . . heard it on the television. Was he yours?"

"He was," Carter said. "But I got the goods."

Both of them seemed to be speaking to the room in general without looking at each other. At the bar, one of the hookers studied them as she stubbed out her cigarette.

"What have you got for me?" Carter asked.

"Look over the menu."

Carter picked up the menu. Inside was a narrow white envelope. His eyes flickered around the room. The woman at the bar was applying a fresh coat of lipstick. The others in the club were absorbed with themselves.

Carter slipped the envelope into his inside jacket pocket.

"That's a bio on this Borassa," Shalinov said. "He's a very mean and dangerous man, highly trained." Here the Russian took a deep drag on his cigar and chuckled dryly. "We trained him."

"Anything on Colonel Muldane?" Carter asked.

"Yes. He's living with a tart in Venice. The address is

in the envelope. Speaking of tarts . . . ."

Carter looked up. The hooker was moving toward them from the bar. She wore a gaudy red dress that clung to the curves and hollows of her hips. She had the kind of full body that looked better covered than not. Her hair was dark, the face strong but not pretty.

"Buona sera . . ."

Neither man spoke.

She stopped, pressing her pubic bone against the table edge. Gently she began rubbing herself against the table, smiling at them. At the same time, she leaned forward. There was a purse under her right hand. She unsnapped the clasp and smiled directly at Carter.

The Killmaster glanced at Shalinov. "Yours?"

The man nodded. "I thought it wise not to carry the goods myself."

Carter slipped the oilskin pouch from beneath his cummerbund. He had already put the ring inside, along with the notebook. The pouch was scarcely inside the purse when she snapped it shut.

"Cheap bastard!" she sneered in a loud voice, and wiggled back to the bar.

"I'll go to Venice early in the morning," Carter said. "If all goes well with Muldune, I should be back by early evening."

Shalinov shrugged. "I'll work the rest of the night, but there are no guarantees. Be here at eight. If I've cracked, make a date with her. She will bring you to me."

"Good enough. Are you in touch with Mock?"

"Of course."

"Then I'll give you my list of hardware to pass on." Without another word, Carter dropped a bill on the table and headed for the door.

On the street he took the same zigzag pattern back to the hotel.

At the reception desk, he checked for messages. There

weren't any, and he toyed with the idea of checking with
Washington and passing on the contents of the envelope
before going up to his room. But it was almost two in
the morning and his brain had begun to grow cobwebs.

The hell with it, he thought, and headed for the
elevator.

Light poured from beneath the door to his room.

It could be that the maid had left the light on when
she turned down the bed.

Or it could be . . .

He unlimbered Wilhelmina, turned the key in the
lock, and pushed the door wide.

"Buona sera, you bastard."

Making herself at home on the far twin bed was
Noreen Parris.

"So, once I got it out of Maria that you had mentioned Milan on the phone and that you were talking to
Maury Richland, I made some phone calls of my own."

"And called every hotel in Milan?"

"That's right," Noreen said sweetly, sitting up to accept one of the two drinks Carter had poured from a
bottle on the dresser.

Her body, in bra and panties, gleamed through the
sheer material of her negligee. Seeing it, Carter remembered her naked and bound on the bed. Against his better instincts, he felt aroused.

On the floor, near the dresser, her bag was open and
half empty. He crossed the closet and found her clothes
hanging beside his.

"You're moving in?"

"The night concierge was very susceptible to a
bribe." She smiled coyly. "Especially when I told him
that you were a policeman and my husband was your
superior and we didn't dare check in together."

Carter just shook his head and swallowed half his
drink. "You're tenacious, Parris, I'll give you that."

She rolled to her knees and sat back on her calves. The way she sat, head slightly cocked to one side, breasts jutting, silken hair falling gently to her shoulders, made her even more appealing.

Carter stifled the impulse to reach out and touch her, and seated himself across the room.

"I want a truce," she said.

"What kind of a truce?"

"I stay out of your hair, but tag along and get the exclusive."

"No deal."

"Then I'll stay in your hair, Nick." She looked at him intently, and then smiled. "Wouldn't it be easier the other way?"

She had a point. He would rather have her where he could see her and make sure she wouldn't screw anything up.

She sensed his thoughts. "I can help, I swear I can. I've got contacts, and I swear you're the boss. I write no more until you say it's a deal."

Carter stared at her for a long moment. "I wish I could believe you."

She stood, moved across the room, and curled onto the arm of his chair. He felt his tiredness ebbing and a surge of desire course through his body.

Desire was the last thing he thought he would feel for Noreen Parris. But, God, he thought, she was beautiful.

"I promise, Nick, your rules," she murmured.

"Okay," he sighed. "I'll try it for forty-eight hours."

"Super. Did you meet Richland?"

"Yeah."

"And you got the notebook back?"

"Yeah."

"That's wonderful!"

"No, not so wonderful. Richland's dead."

She paled. "My God."

"At the opera house. A piano wire garrote around his

neck. You still want to follow me around?''

In reply, she bounded from the chair, crossed to the wall switch, and dimmed the lights to an eerie glow. She turned to face him. "I want to do more than that.''

He had half-expected it, but it still surprised the hell out of him.

Without blinking, she let the negligee slip to the floor. Her arms slid up her back and the bra came away.

"Are you just going to sit there?" she whispered.

"For the time being," he said with a smile, sipping his drink.

She took off her panties, flipped them into his lap, and followed them.

"I'd still let you tag along without this, you know," he said.

"I was hoping you'd say that. But, believe me, Nick, this has nothing to do with business.''

She settled into the chair. He could feel her warm rump settling heavily against his thigh. She leaned forward and gently brushed her lips back and forth over his as her hands moved along his shirt front, opening the buttons.

"I think you'll discover I'm not the ice cube you think I am," she murmured, nuzzling his ear.

"I'm getting a pretty good hint.''

The warmth of her naked body seemed to flow between them, and the scent of her perfume was making him slightly dizzy.

He felt her lips nibbling on his neck and her fingers curling into the hair on his chest. She nestled harder against him in the chair, taking the glass from his hand, leaning over to place it on the lamp table.

One white breast, brown-tipped, provocative, brushed his cheek.

"Bitch," he moaned.

"Bastard," she sighed, her hand on his chest, her fingers pulling gently but with an underlying ferocity at the thick mat of curling hair, a hint of erotic violence in her knowing hands.

He sat up and she pressed hard against him, fitting her body to his. She took his hand and placed it over her bare breast. He felt the warm softness of it, the hammering of her heart, and the fluid juices of desire began to fill him. Their lips came together in a fierce kiss.

As their mouths parted, she fitted herself to him. They sat side by side, facing one another. He felt her hungry lips on his chest, nibbling, just before she crushed her firm, provocative breasts against him.

"You have too damned many clothes on," she breathed.

Suddenly they were on their feet and her hands were flying over his body, skillfully divesting him of his clothing.

When he was as naked as she, she pulled him to the bed, her lips burning on his shoulder. He was aroused. He pressed against her, feeling the springiness of her body, the strength. It was as though they were wrestling. Her arms were muscular and quick, strapping him to her. He rolled to one side and she rolled with him. Her breasts pushed into his chest, soft and pointed, her large, dark nipples glistening with perspiration.

"Kiss them!" she implored tersely.

It was an order, but kissing was precisely what he had wanted to do. He lowered his face to her straining breasts, felt the soft round globes graze his cheek as he moved his mouth from one to the other, his lips parted, his tongue moistening the warm, pulsing flesh. Then her hands guided him until he found and caressed a hot, upright nipple.

"Oh, God, yes . . . that's it!" she cried through clenched teeth.

Carter felt her whole body tremble, and then she was writhing beneath him, pulling him down to her, clamping him within the circle of her tightening thighs. A shiver went through him as their bodies touched and seemed to melt together in a shuddering embrace.

Then they were rolling and suddenly she was on top. Nestling her head on his chest, she took a nibble from his ear. Carter felt her tongue slip down his neck, the fiery sensation spreading across his chest. He found her buttocks and rubbed them gently. She spread her legs until they straddled his, and they both slid down in the bed. Her tongue moved playfully around his lips. He was conscious of his groin pushing up urgently, finally penetrating her, the warmth saturating his body. His hands slid through her hair as they kissed.

"So good. So . . . good . . ." she murmured, breathing in his ear.

The spiral of pleasure spread up his belly as his muscles tightened. Their hips moved in tandem, smoothly, without effort. The sensation built irresistibly in his groin. There was a sweet aching in his ribs. His hands swung out to seize her bottom again, thrusting inside her until she was tight against him.

"Oh, yes . . . yes!"

She bit into his shoulder, her arms wrapped around his neck. The tugging in his stomach suddenly eased, then tightened again. He felt himself losing control. The explosion made him shudder. She moaned softly, her teeth digging further into his flesh.

Finally—it seemed like minutes later—she was beside him, sighing and curling her satiated body against his.

"Where do we go tomorrow?"

"I go to Venice," he replied. "You stay here by the phone. My code man just might crack the notebook early and call. Any argument?"

"None," she replied, as her hands and lips went back to work on his body.

TWELVE

On the short flight from Milan to Venice, Carter devoured the two-page bio on Jacob Borassa. It made interesting reading.

During the reign of Idi Amin in Uganda, torture and elimination were taken to new heights. All of it was done under the direction of the State Research Bureau, Amin's secret police.

An integral arm of the Research Bureau—and probably its most feared until—was called the Striker Unit.

The task of the Striker Unit was primarily elimination, and it was directly responsible to President Amin. The pattern of operation was well documented, as were most of its higher-ranking officers.

Jacob Borassa had held the rank of lieutenant colonel in the military police at Makindye Prison. It was generally believed that Borassa was the head of the Striker Unit in the last days of Amin.

But before his rise with Amin, Borassa had attended Patrice Lumumba University in Moscow, as well as the KGB school in Kiev.

The bio answered a lot of questions and raised others. Could Borassa himself be Ala-Din Mohammed? So far, most of the principals uncovered in the One Hundred Eyes were from Uganda and they originated in the Vezzine tribe. Were the Vezzines and the One Hundred Eyes interchangeable?'

Carter guessed that it was a safe bet. As for Borassa being Ala-Din Muhammed, he doubted it. Whoever the real person was behind the reincarnation of the old desert tyrant, he wouldn't stoop to getting his hands dirty doing the kind of field work Jacob Borassa was doing.

When the plane landed at Marco Polo di Tessera Airport, Carter put a scrambler call through to Washington.

CIA and NSA researchers had come up with just about the same material and background on Borassa as Carter had gotten from General Mock.

On a hunch, the Killmaster requested a complete rundown on Amin's general staff, particularly those men, and even women, who were peers or immediate superiors of Borassa.

He requested the material posthaste, to be delivered to the hotel in Milan by special messenger.

This done, he boarded a water taxi for the eight-mile canal ride into the city.

The every-morning fog was nearly burned off and the wind from Trieste smelled like rain. Along the Grand Canal, the stacks of trestles and duckboards were standing in readiness for the high tides of afternoon.

Carter stepped ashore at the Riva degli Schiavoni, and walked across the Piazza San Marco to the narrow end. Just across Via Dell'Ascensione, he entered the Frezzeria, an area where twenty-four hours a day there is Venetian *dolce far niente*—sweet idleness.

It would be just like Trig Muldune to live in this section where the norm is painted women, padded checks, and watered liquor.

The address was easy to find, a crumbling four-story

brick building on a tiny street barely wide enough for
two people to pass.

All the apartments were floor-throughs. Muldune occupied the second floor. As Carter mounted the creaking, foul-smelling stairs he heard a verbal battle royal
taking place just above him, and recognized Muldune's
heavy bass voice.

At the head of the stairs he paused. The wide double
doors to the apartment were open.

A tall, striking woman with dripping wet black hair
and a voluptuous figure stood in front of a full-length
mirror.

At her feet were a towel and a sopping wet black
dress. She was wearing slacks and a brassiere, the strap
wide and white across her olive-toned back.

"What are you doing?" the woman suddenly
screamed, sweeping jars and tubes of makeup from the
dressing table before her into a vanity case.

"What the fuck do you care?" came Muldune's voice
from somewhere on the other side of the room.

"I don't, pig!"

"I'm opening another bottle of whiskey."

"Typical," she spat in staccato Italian. "All you've
done since I've known you is drink, drink, drink!"

"With you around, what else is there to do?"

The woman gave him the age-old sign with a raised
right arm, and stooped to pick up a sweater from a pile
of clothing near the wet dress. She slid it over her head
and settled the bottom over her hips. With abrupt,
angry gestures, she rolled the turtleneck beneath her
chin.

"You know murder is against the law," she rasped,
running a comb through her damp, dark hair.

"I didn't murder you. You're alive."

"You threw me in the canal!" she shrieked.

"To cool you off."

Suddenly, Muldune appeared at her side, a bottle in

one hand and a glass in the other. He was nearly six inches shorter than the woman, but dwarfed her in width. In a tank-style undershirt and tight dungarees, he looked like every young weightlifter would like to look at twenty, much less Muldune's forty.

"You're not really leavin' old Trig now, are ya, darlin'?"

"There's a train in forty minutes to Milan. From there a plane to Rome. I'm going to be on it."

Muldune shrugged and moved to a nearby counter. "Well, I've but one thing to say . . . don't let the doorknob hit you in the ass on the way out, darlin'."

Steaming, she knelt down and snapped her suitcase shut. She picked up a thin summer coat from an arm-chair and slid into it. Then she stormed to the door and paused, obviously trying to come up with an exit line.

"You know," Muldune said conversationally, "you look a million times better when you're angry. That's the way I've always wanted to photograph you . . . mean, moody, and malevolent."

She screamed like a banshee and then found words. "And you know what you can do with your cameras, bastard! And your tripod, too!" She flounced past Carter with a toss of her head without even seeing him.

The Killmaster waited for the clatter of her heels to recede down the stairs, and then stepped into the door-way.

Muldune was at the counter, pouring a large glass of whiskey and topping it with San Pellegrino.

"Got another one of those?"

Animal instinct took over the instant Carter spoke. Muldune whirled, the neck of the bottle in his hammy fist. His eyes widened, blinked, and then squinted as a wide smile of recognition creased his lips.

"My God, it's the bloody boogeyman! What brings you to this armpit, ol' Nick?"

"You," Carter replied, crossing the room to be caught in a bear hug.

"It's good to see you're still alive, old sod. Here, take this one. It's the only glass. That bitch broke the rest of 'em on my head."

Muldune raised the bottle in a toast and drank from it. Carter sipped, coughed, and lit a cigarette.

"Sorry to come in on your domestic situation."

Muldune shrugged and laughed. "It's better she's gone. Another six months and we would have killed each other. Lovely lass in the sack, but she's got this queer need to have the bills paid on time."

Carter had already let his eyes roam the apartment. The adjoining room had been rigged up like a studio, with cameras and tripods and backdrops.

"Photography?"

"It's a good cover for my other enterprises," Muldune grinned. "Only trouble is, the other enterprises are a little slack right now."

"Would you like a vacation trip . . . a little working vacation?"

Both men eyed each other and broke into smiles.

Without being asked, Carter laid out in a simple, quick explanation what he planned to do with the ex-SAS man's part in it.

"Borassa and the Vezzines, huh?" Muldune murmured when he had finished. "They're bloody mean buggers, they are. They're like simbas with brains."

"You know Borassa?"

"Ran into him now and then. He ran the torture camps for Macías down in Guinea after he left Uganda."

"Is that so?" Carter mused aloud. That piece of information hadn't been in the Moscow or the Washington file.

Macías, appointed president for life of Equatorial

Guinea in 1972, had turned the once peaceful and prosperous West African nation into a concentration camp where torture, murder, and forced labor became national policy. He was personally responsible for fifty thousand deaths, and many African heads of state privately referred to Equatorial Guinea as the Auschwitz of Africa.

Muldune was still speaking, and something he said made Carter tune back in.

". . . of course, a lot of them that ran from Uganda ended up in Equatorial Guinea, you know."

"No, I didn't know," Carter replied.

"Figures—those gentlemen didn't advertise. Hell, even Amin's Hajib Tutambe ended up down there. He was the boy who specialized in facial razor cuts treated with meat tenderizer."

Carter's brain was going just a little over Mach 1 at this point.

"Trig, do you have a phone?"

"Yeah, right there, if you can get the bleedin' thing to work."

Carter got it to work, and told Washington to check out the death by firing squad of one of the most hated men in Africa, Hajib Tutambe.

If Tutambe were still alive, he would fit the profile of Ala-Din Muhammed like a second skin.

When he hung up and turned to face Muldune, the man had changed clothes and stood now with a small black satchel in one hand, the ever-present bottle of whiskey in the other.

Carter grinned. "I take it you're in."

"You take it right, ol' sod."

"Don't you want to know the pay?"

"It's got to be a bleedin' sight more than I'm makin' now. Shall we go?"

It was a two-hour wait at the airport for a Milan

plane. In that time, the two men put together everything
they knew between them about Jacob Borassa and Hajib Tutambe. Muldune was even able to add a few more
names that were completely new to Carter.

By the time the plane set down at Milan's Malpensa
Airport, Carter was pretty sure he had laid out on a
legal pad the ruling structure of the One Hundred Eyes.

He was also pretty sure he now knew why the KGB
and General Mock were so eager to help him nail the
men behind the group.

The bar was the same, as were the bartender, the
waitress, and the hookers. The female contact tossed an
eyebrow at Carter when he entered, but played come-
hither games from the bar for a full ten minutes while
the Killmaster sipped a whiskey.

It was exactly eight o'clock, three hours since they
had arrived back at the hotel in Milan. Carter had arranged for Muldune to have the adjoining room to his
and Noreen's. The fact that the famous female reporter
was in on the gig hardly fazed Muldune. He had worked
with the Killmaster several times in the past and trusted
his decisions.

Over a room service dinner, they debated the twenty-
odd pages that had been messengered from Washington. They would need proof, of course, but they all
decided that, if Hajib Tutambe's death had been faked
right after Macías's fall in Guinea, he was definitely
their man.

His dossier read like a master plan from hell, and the
personality that emerged qualified the man to be Satan
himself.

Over brandy, Carter and Muldune drew up a shop-
ping list of small arms and other ordnance they would
need.

Then, just before taking off to meet Serge Shalinov's

contact, Carter had a call in the room. It was Mock, instructing him to call back from the pay phone in the hotel lobby.

"What's up?"

"You have your ordnance list?"

"Yes."

"Give it to me," Mock had replied, an uncustomary tenseness in his voice.

Carter did, and added, "I'm heading Shalinov's way now."

"I know. Make sure you get all the material. Leave no copies."

This had given Carter a bit of a shock. KGB generals usually cover their butts by having copies spread around. Carter made a stab. "Are you having trouble with your people?"

"Let us say I am trying to avoid it."

Carter had hung up and headed for the meet a good deal more confused than he had been earlier in the day.

"Buy a lady a drink?"

"Sure," Carter replied, and signaled the waitress.

It wasn't the same dress, but this one did the same things to her body. She moved into the booth beside Carter and did a number on his left bicep with her breasts until the drink came.

As she sipped her drink, they bartered over price in voices just loud enough to be heard by the other girls. Once that was settled, they lowered their voices to whispers.

"Has he cracked it?" Carter asked.

"Yes. He was breaking it all down when I left him about an hour ago. It should be ready by the time we get there."

They dawdled over their drinks for another fifteen minutes. Carter was getting impatient. "Is all this caution necessary?"

She shrugged. "My orders. Serge thinks he was followed from here last night. Be very sexy on the way out.''

They moved casually toward the door. When she slipped her arm around his waist, Carter did the same.

About a block from the bar, she tugged him into a little recess between the two buildings.

"Kiss me!"

Carter pulled her close and kissed her. She responded the minute his lips touched hers, and clung to him like a leech as his hands moved up and down her back. When she broke it, she whispered in his ear, "We are being followed. Two men in the next block, a black Fiat."

"C'mon!"

They moved on down the street, still entwined. Carter slipped on the eyeglasses and adjusted them.

She was right. The black Fiat began to crawl along behind them, keeping its distance. He couldn't see clearly the features of the two men in the front seat, but he could recognize that they were white.

"What shall we do?"

"Nothing," Carter growled.

"But we can't lead them to Serge."

"I think we can," he replied, tightening his hold.

It was another eight blocks, and the Fiat did nothing but trail.

"In here!"

Carter followed her into a building indistinguishable from twenty others on the block. They climbed to the third floor and she rapped on a paint-peeling door.

Behind it, Carter could hear a computer printer chattering away.

Shalinov opened the door and they darted inside. It was a sparsely furnished room, its center occupied by a large desk, the desk illuminated brightly by an overhead light. On the desk was a portable computer, and beside it a printer. The printer was going like hell and there was a three-inch pile of finished copy already stacked.

"We were followed," the woman said. "He wouldn't let me get rid of them."

"Who?" Shalinov said, whirling on Carter.

"I didn't see their faces, but that's not important now. This stuff is. How much do you have to go?"

"It's nearly finished. I—"

"Have you had a chance to go over it?"

"No. I just broke it and fed it into the machine."

The machine came to an abrupt halt and Carter rolled up the platen. When the printed pages were rolled and under his belt, he tapped the button on the computer that released the floppy disc. This joined the pages.

"Where's the notebook and the ring?"

"There, but wait. I have to make a copy for files and for General Mock."

Carter pocketed the notebook and the ring and filled his hand with Wilhelmina.

"You can tell Mock that he's been screwed. Is there a back way out?"

Silence. Carter put two inches of the Luger's barrel into the man's belly. "Is there?"

"Fire escape, end of the hall. I don't understand. Comrade Mock told us to cooperate with you."

Carter chuckled. "Even General Mock can make mistakes."

One solid chop to the side of the neck, and Shalinov dropped to the floor like a felled tree. The woman posed no threat. She stood shaking by the door, her mouth catching flies.

"Take off your pantyhose!"

No argument.

Carter tied her ankles to her wrists behind her. He ripped the telephone cord from the wall and sprinted down the hall toward the rear of the building. The window opened easily and he slid through it. Instead of going down the fire escape, he went up, to the roof. He padded to the front, dropped to his belly, and eased his eyes over.

The black Fiat was parked across the street. He could see the glow of cigarettes through the window. The Killmaster forced his body to relax into a waiting stance. It was just a question of what happened first: the woman struggling out of the pantyhose or Shalinov waking up.

It took fifteen minutes. Both of them rolled out of the front door. At the same time, two men bounced out of the Fiat.

Carter eyeballed them hard as they crossed the street: wide, Slavic faces above stocky bodies in suits that hadn't been pressed in a month.

If they ain't KGB, Carter thought dryly, *I'm an elf in the Black Forest*.

The surprise on the woman's and Shalinov's face completed the picture. The code man actually hadn't known who was tailing them.

Carter couldn't make out what they were saying, but a word or two told him that they were speaking Russian.

The shorter and wider of the two—if that were possible—peeled away and headed for the alley at the rear of the building and the fire escape. The other ushered Shalinov and the woman into the Fiat.

The AXE agent padded to the back of the building and stretched out again. Short and Thick reconned the area around the fire escape and both ends of the alley. After a few minutes he seemed satisfied that Carter had flown, and headed back to the Fiat.

Carter watched him exchange a few words with his comrade and get in the passenger seat. The Fiat sped away. He waited the full length of a cigarette, then trotted back down to the apartment that Shalinov was using for an office. Five minutes later he had the telephone repaired and was dialing the hotel.

Noreen Parris answered the hotel operator's first ring. "Hello?"

"Me. This number is 484-115. Call me back from a lobby phone, pronto."

He hung up and used the time to assure himself that there was nothing that could be used from the room. It was as clean as a pin.

When the phone rang he grabbed it. "Noreen?"

"Yes."

"You're on the ball, lady—stay that way. Get Trig and check out of the hotel. Take my bag with you. He'll know where to get a car this time of night. Drive to Nice. There's one flight a day from Nice to Cagliari, Sardinia, with a stop on Corsica. Got that?"

"You want us to drive to Nice and fly to Cagliari, Sardinia."

"Brilliant," Carter countered. "Check into the Hotel Mediterraneo. I should be able to join you day after tomorrow."

"You mean you're not even coming back to the hotel here?"

"You guessed it. 'Bye."

He hung up and redialed the number he had used before for Mock. The general himself picked up on the first ring.

"I gather, Comrade General, that you are no longer on the *Smoldosk*."

"No. I thought I could further our little adventure with less interference if I operated on my own."

"We have a saying . . . bullshit. Are your people crawling your back?"

There was a long pause, during which Carter could have sworn he could hear the tumblers in the other man's mind turning.

"Why do you ask?"

"Because Shalinov had two of your types on him.

They picked him and his female go-between up right after I picked up the finished goods."

"You got everything?"

"Yeah, all of it. And I laid a scent that I was double-crossing you and taking the action all for myself."

"I appreciate that, Nick." There was little doubt of the relief in the other man's voice.

"You want to tell me what's going on, General?"

There was another long pause before he spoke again. "There are certain documents—records of payments, that sort of thing—being held by the One Hundred Eyes. Moscow would like those documents kept quiet . . ."

"So they've ordered you off."

"So it would seem."

"Those documents wouldn't have to do with the Soviet and KGB backing of Macías in Equatorial Guinea, would they?"

The sigh from the other end of the line was not ex-asperation. It was more resignation. "I only learned about it earlier today."

Now it was clear. The world only suspected that most of the carnage in Guinea before Macías's overthrow had been financed and engineered by the Soviets. Evidently, the leadership of the One Hundred Eyes had conclusive proof, and was using it for blackmail.

Carter said so.

Mock agreed.

"So Moscow is willing to let well enough alone," Carter said. "Even though they've lost as many to this madman as we have, they want to let him go on?"

"So it would seem."

"Hajib Tutambe is Ala-Din Muhammed, isn't he?"

"I don't know for sure," Mock replied, "but my guess is yes."

"He blackmailed them before with what he had, and

your people faked his death, not realizing that when he resurfaced he planned on throwing all of us out of Africa.''

The voice was flat now, a dull monotone. ''That's the way I've put it together, yes. But I swear, Nick, I've only put it together in the last few hours.''

Carter took time to light a cigarette and take a few deep drags. ''So, which way do you go?''

''Two of those he killed on our side were old friends, lifelong friends. If he gets away with it, what I do becomes meaningless.''

''Yeah, and if you stay with it, you might need that little piece of Arizona. Are you willing to risk it?''

''I've already decided. Yes.''

''I'm going to trust you, General, because I have to. Washington wants the problem solved, but, like Moscow, they don't want to get their hands dirty. Have you got the hardware?''

''I do.''

''Where are you now?''

''Kuwait.''

''Can you get yourself and the equipment to Cagliari, Sardinia, by day after tomorrow?''

''It will be difficult, but, yes, I can do it.''

''I'll see you there, the Hotel Mediterraneo.''

Carter hung up and made the street. The fourth cab he spotted was fairly new, and the medallion on the window told him that the driver was an independent, which meant he could go just about anywhere he wanted.

''*Sí, signore?*''

''Genoa, the airport.''

''*Where?*'' the driver asked, whirling in the seat.

''Genoa,'' Carter repeated.

''But, signore, we have an airport here in Milan.''

''I know,'' Carter said, smiling. ''But my wife watches for me at the Milan airport, so I'm flying out of Genoa to meet my mistress.''

THIRTEEN

The Killmaster got a late-night flight out of Genoa to Rome. Using his diplomatic passport at Leonardo da Vinci so that Wilhelmina and Hugo could be passed through to travel with him, he made a reservation once again in the Fields name for a morning flight to Barcelona, then found a hotel near the airport and crashed.

The plane left at ten. Carter's internal alarm clock went off at eight sharp. He ordered a room service breakfast, and tipped the waiter heavily to go out and buy him a new shirt, underwear, socks, and toilet articles.

By the time he had eaten and showered, the waiter was back. Carter tipped him again, shaved, and dressed. He gauged the time so he arrived exactly a half hour before flight time.

A quick look around the boarding area told him there were no bad guys. He hung back and was the last first-class passenger to board.

Once in the air, fortified with fresh coffee, he dug into the papers that Shalinov had decoded.

They were every bit as valuable as he had guessed, and more. General Mock had guessed right about Berbera in Somalia, and three of the other stations in

Namibia, Swaziland, and Ethiopia. He had missed
about Accra in Ghana. Instead of Ghana, another station was a few countries down, outside Bata, in Equatorial Guinea. The fortress, presumably in the Air
Mountains of Niger, was referred to only as Home
Base.

There were simply code keys for telephone transmissions, presumably for field agents, master modem
numbers for computer traffic, and cipher keys for radio
communication.

Carter smiled to himself as he tucked the papers
away. With what he now had, all they needed to do was
take one of the stations intact. Once that was done, it
would be only a matter of listening and waiting until
they could pinpoint both the fortress and the location of
the One Hundred Eyes financing.

And once that was done, it was move-in time.

The moment he cleared customs, he found a telephone directory with the number and address of La
Muñequita Papel.

"Could I speak to Señor Hardy, *por favor*?"

"He is not in, señor."

"What time does he arrive?"

"Not until eight this evening."

"*Gracias.*"

Carter cabbed to the Plaza de Cataluña at the top of
the Ramblas. Once there, he bought some fresh clothes
for himself, and a suitcase, and located a specialty shop
that catered to the church.

"*Buenos dias, señor.* May I help you?"

"Yes, I would like to buy a present for my sister . . . a
nun's habit."

The young, dark-eyed clerk barely blinked an eye.
"What size, señor?"

"About two sizes larger than you would wear. And
I'll need everything that goes with it . . . cowl, rosary,
everything."

A half hour later he walked further down the Ramblas carrying the suitcase and the clothing box. At the Calle del Carmen, he turned right and checked into a small hotel using the Fields passport.

A half hour after checking in, he was sound asleep.

La Muñequita Papel was a splashy, two-story joint complete with a doorman off the Plaza Calvo Sotelo. The garish Vegas-type neon signs outside advertised *Girls! Girls! Girls!* and *Espectáculos Sexy*.

"This is fine," Carter said, and dropped a large bill over the seat.

The cab pulled away and Carter leaned against a lamppost, lighting a cigarette and watching the patrons come and go. He also checked the street for anyone loitering like himself.

It was clean, but he had already decided not to take a chance. If Mock's people were checking back on his "information requests," Hardy's name might have popped up. The KGB was slow, but they were thorough. By now they could have someone in the club.

Carter had already determined that the only person he wanted to see or identify himself to was the man himself.

He stayed on the opposite side of the street and meandered toward the joint. The building was separated from its neighbors by a lane not more than two feet wide.

Next door as he approached was a closed boutique with a lighted window display. Carter paused in front of it, pretending an interest in the overdressed mannequins, while he studied the second-floor windows.

That's where the offices would be, he figured, and if he knew Hardy, that's where ol' Ace would be—letting the action take care of itself on the first floor while he wheeled and dealed on the second.

There were two windows lit on the second floor, a corner rear and a corner front. The drapes were drawn on the rear windows.

That was the one Carter chose to go for.

He waited for a moment while the doorman helped a couple of drunks into a cab. The rest of the street was deserted. Quickly, he darted into the slot between the buildings and made his way to the back.

There was an alley entrance to the kitchen, as he had been certain there would be, the door standing invitingly ajar and with the brightly lighted kitchen on the left. Carter paused outside the door and watched a chef stirring a huge pot of soup on the range while two busboys came staggering in under heavy trays that they clatteringly unloaded at the sink beyond his line of vision.

Choosing a moment when no one faced in his direction, Carter entered and went unhurriedly past the open kitchen door, following a dimly lit hall to a closed wooden door at the end. It was locked, but he took the knob firmly and braced himself, putting steady and increasing pressure with his shoulder against the door, and the flimsy catch gave way. His tight hold of the doorknob prevented him from catapulting forward, and he found himself in the narrow corridor with the flight of stairs leading upward.

Hot music and the laughter and din of a nightspot doing good business came at him with a rush from the other end of the corridor as Carter closed the door behind him. At the far end toward the front he saw the back of a giant with his back to the corridor.

He had the look of being posted there as a guard to prevent entrance to the stairway, and this gave Carter further hope that his rear window guess was right.

He climbed the stairs swiftly and quietly, and found himself in a short hallway with three doors on his left.

From the second door he heard the loud voice he knew so well barking orders into an intercom. It wouldn't do to walk straight in there. Ace didn't like surprises.

He tried the first door. It opened, and Carter stepped into a darkened office with desks and filing cabinets.

There was a connecting door, and through it the Killmaster saw the man hunched over a littered desk the size of the *Titanic*. Even from the back there was no mistaking who it was.

Carter eased the door open and made sure he was a good target before he spoke.

"Putting a little weight on, aren't you, Ace?"

The big man started with surprise, and then visibly relaxed. "Hello, Nick!" he said with a broad smile as he swiveled in his chair and stood.

Ace Hardy looked like Genghis Khan should have looked. Only Genghis couldn't have been as mean. Hardy's shaved head glistened, his black Mandarin mustache drooped to his chest, and his mammoth body had to be in good shape to hold up all the gold around his neck.

"How are ya, ya sorry bastard?" he thundered, nearly cracking Carter's shoulder blade with a friendly clap on the back.

"Thirsty."

"There's one poured for ya, just add the cube."

Carter followed the jerk of Hardy's head. On a sideboard stood a glass with three fingers in it and a bottle of newly opened Chivas.

"You were expecting me?" Carter said, dropping a cube in the glass and savoring a long swallow.

"Two ways. Earlier this evening, a couple of stiff-backed suits waltzed in here flashing Interpol badges. They say they're looking for ya. I ask, What for? They say, It's classified. I tell 'em I don't know ya. They say they think I do and there are ways to get my cooperation. I say, 'Screw the both of ya,' and I kick their asses down the stairs."

"They weren't Interpol," Carter said, easing himself onto the edge of the desk.

"You think I don't know that? Christ, I'm on a first-name basis with every Interpol fieldman in Spain for the last five years."

"How was their Spanish?"

" 'Bout like mine—lousy. I think they were German."

Carter nodded. "Ten to one East German."

"You're still in the game, then?"

"In a way." Carter smiled. "What about number two?"

"Last night my cook adds a black kid from Morocco to the cleanup crew. This morning I find a bug on my phone. I got good people. It had to be him. I don't put the two of 'em together until the suits come in."

Carter was interested. "Will the kid come in again tonight?"

"He already did. I hit him with your name and he says he don't know shit. You know how I read people. He's lyin'. So I break his arm."

"And?"

"And he don't say shit. Tough little bastard."

"Where is he now?"

"A little holding room I got in the front."

That would explain the front-corner light, Carter thought. "Can I try?"

"Sure. This way."

Hardy led the way out of the office and opened a panel in an otherwise blank wall opposite. At the end of a long, second hall, he came up with a set of keys and opened the only door in the hall.

"Well, I'll be damned . . ."

He wasn't over twenty, and was still dressed in busboy whites. He was tied, arms and legs, to a narrow cot. His mouth gaped open and his eyes stared at nothing.

Before Carter even touched the side of his neck, he knew he would find no pulse.

Deftly, he ran his finger around inside and over the tongue, and came out with a tooth.

"Hollow," Carter growled, and smelled the cavity. "Cyanide capsule."

Without a word, Hardy moved to a nearby table and

picked up a phone. In fractured Spanish he informed someone down below in the club that there was a package upstairs that had to be deposited in the bay. When he was sure he had made himself clear, he hung up and turned to Carter.

"Want to tell me what the hell this is all about?"

"Sure," the Killmaster said. "Want to buy me another drink?"

Among many other things, Ace Hardy made his money watching other people make fools out of themselves on the booze he sold them. For this reason he didn't drink himself.

By the time Carter finished telling him the whole story, the big man crossed to the sideboard and poured himself a stiff whiskey.

"So this Mock is in the shithouse, and his KGB pals are playing footsie with this Hundred Eyes outfit to keep them quiet?"

"That's my guess," Carter said, nodding. "Your busboy probably takes his orders from Tutambe. The only way the One Hundred Eyes could have found out I was headed for you was a KGB leak after Mock put out the word I wanted your location."

Hardy sipped from his glass and put a few hundred creases in his shiny forehead as he sifted it all.

"You're pretty sure nobody nailed you coming into Barcelona or coming here?"

"Positive."

He poked a button on his desk. "Okay, whether we do business or not, I think you've got to be expressed out of town. What was that hotel?"

"The Odella, on Calle del Carmen."

"Gimme your key."

Carter handed it over about the time the giant from below slipped into the room. Hardy barked orders that Carter's bags were to be picked up and brought back to the club. "Also, have Papa get the *Sea Breeze* ready.

He's takin' a little sail down to Valencia about midnight."

The giant nodded, caught the room key in a fist as big as Carter's head, and bowed out of the room.

"Good man," Hardy chuckled. "Can't pronounce his Basque name, so I call him Olaf the Terrible." He eased himself into the chair behind the desk and peered at Carter through the pyramid of his fingers. "Okay, my man, run this stuff by me one more time."

Carter moved around to his side of the desk and referred to the map spread before them. "You deal with the Bedouins who know the trails in this part of the Sahara, right?"

"If you're sayin' that my Bedouin friends transport anything illegal, forget it. If you're sayin' I am helping the economy of a Third World people . . . right."

Carter smiled. He knew that the Bedouins could go anywhere in that desert, even Libya, without being bothered. He also knew that Ace Hardy had been supplying them with contraband for years.

"Let's put it this way, Ace . . . your desert 'friends' will do whatever you ask." The man shrugged, and Carter continued, a finger pointing to a spot on the map. "You've got a radio station, here, in southern Morocco. If we take their station here—in Somalia— and one other over here—in Guinea—we can cross signals in the triangle and pinpoint Home Base."

"That would take a direction-finding unit with one hell of a lot of boost. I don't have one down there."

"Can you get one?" Carter asked.

"Expensive."

"Cost is no object."

This brought out a wide grin. "Music to my ears, my man. Go on!"

"Once we've set up the location of the fortress, we move in with a Bedouin caravan and waste the place. That is, after we monitor their traffic to find out what we can hijack, and substitute our Bedouins for their couriers. The fortress has to be supplied. My guess is out of one of the larger towns in Niger. One of those is our best bet.''

Hardy leaned forward and silently studied the map for a full ten minutes. At last he spoke. ''What's in it for me and my associates?''

''You name it. If we intercept the kind of traffic I think we will, we can nail all their bank accounts. It should be quite a tidy sum.''

''Money isn't my problem right now,'' Hardy replied, leaning back in the chair.

''What is?''

''In the basement of this club are certain games of chance. I also have basements such as this in Marbella, Madrid, and Seville. About a year ago, because of a slight misunderstanding, my licenses were lifted.''

Carter grinned. ''Ace, you drive a hard bargain.''

The big man shrugged. ''I have stockholders.''

''Where's your phone?''

It was nearly an hour before Carter got a call back from Washington.

''Your case will be reviewed in two weeks' time. The fine should be in the neighborhood of fifty thou, American.''

''Cheap enough,'' Hardy sighed, moving to the side-board. He played games with the molding, and half the wall swung out to reveal an elaborately equipped radio room.

Carter knew that the room he was seeing connected Hardy to a worldwide smuggling operation . . . casinos, clubs like the one below him, and freighters that didn't ask too much about their cargoes.

The Killmaster whistled. ''Five years brings a lot of changes.''

Hardy chuckled. ''In my business you keep sailing faster or you sink. Excuse me.''

Carter got a fresh drink and moved across the room where he couldn't hear.

Twenty minutes later, Hardy reentered the office and closed the panel behind him.

"We go, but I'll have to make a little run down there. My man, Harun Al-Bidi, doesn't like to commit without an eyeball-to-eyeball meet."

"Fair enough," Carter replied. "Can you be in Cagliari, Sardinia, in forty-eight hours?"

"Shouldn't be too much of a problem. What's there?"

"Rollo. I want to use him and the *Long Shot* to hit Berbera."

"The one-eyed bandit?" Hardy hooted. "I thought he was dead."

"Not yet, but he might be if he's in the can down there much longer."

Hardy roared with laughter as he led Carter down yet another set of back stairs to a deserted part of the kitchen. He opened the door to a walk-in freezer. The opposite wall of the freezer became another door. Through it they walked into the rear of an air-conditioned van. The door was scarcely closed behind them when the van roared away.

Through the tiny porthole window Carter could see that it was the giant, Olaf the Terrible, driving.

"Ace . . ."

"Yeah?"

"How good is this Olaf?"

The big man grinned. "Bad, very bad. Eats mortars and shits forty-five slugs."

"But can he move?"

"So quiet he can work a hotel room and fluff your pillow while he's lifting your wallet."

"Maybe you should being him along," Carter said.

An hour later they were all on Hardy's private forty-foot sloop, the *Sea Breeze*, skirting the coast south toward Valencia.

FOURTEEN

Since the hour was late, the number of cars on the ferry was few. Carter had no more than a ten-minute wait before he was over the ramp and gearing through the narrow, winding streets of Porto Torres. A few minutes later and he had cleared the port village and gained the coastal highway south toward Cagliari.

Above him, the moon had gone and black clouds were piling in from the sea. The wind was warm but surprisingly strong, bringing with it a smattering of rain.

He was slightly behind schedule, but because of Mock's people tapping him, it was expedient to use the extra time.

The morning flight from Valencia to Nice had been uneventful. Carter was sure he hadn't been pegged at the Nice airport, but he made the decision to go the rest of the way by car and ferry instead of plane.

This would also allow him time to see Monsieur René Dufasse.

In Nice, he rented a car from a downtown depot and made a phone call. Dufasse himself answered. Carter identified himself, and made sure that the old forger was still at the same address and still in business.

He drove north to the St. Etienne section and parked

near the train station. A short walk brought him to Rue Marceau and he started checking numbers.

It was a neighborhood for respectable day people—doctors, attorneys, cafés, and many specialty shops. About a block from the square of the Chagall Museum he saw the scrolled sign: Dufasse—Printing.

Carter pushed the door aside and entered. A tiny bell brought a young, girl through a pair of curtains into the front of the shop.

"*Bonjour, monsieur.*" She was dressed in a school pinafore and wore knee-high white socks.

"Monsieur Carter to see Monsieur Dufasse."

She turned toward the doorway, but Dufasse was already stepping through the curtains.

He was in his mid-sixties, about five feet tall, equally as wide, and had a face that could have been Santa Claus without the beard. If it were possible, his bright eyes got even merrier when they saw Carter.

"Ah, Nicholas. *Bonjour, mon ami*!" he exclaimed, and did the French number on both of Carter's cheeks. "Eveline, you must be off to school."

"*Au revoir,*" the girl replied, grabbing a book bag from the counter and kissing the old man before running out the door.

"My niece."

"Lovely," Carter replied.

"This way."

In the print shop proper, fortified with café au lait and croissants, the old man got right down to business.

"What do you need?"

"A passport, American, in the name of Noreen Rowland." Carter handed the old man a sheet of vital statistics on Noreen Parris.

"I see. And what is the woman's occupation to be?"

"Nun. I'll also need church papers of identification."

"That won't be difficult," Dufasse said. "What else?"

"Maritime identification papers for a yacht." Carter

passed over the specs he knew on the *Long Shot*, Rowland's boat.

"What country and home port do you want?"

"Anywhere other than its real one, Nice, France."

"Do you want entry and exit stamps on the passport?"

"Yes. Background stuff, a vacation here and there. Entry tomorrow into Italy."

"When do you need them?"

"I'm taking the ferry to Corsica at two this afternoon."

The twinkling eyes grew round. "My God, Nicholas, that's impossible!" The words came out in a lungy wheeze, like air escaping from a tire.

Carter smiled. "I realize that a shortage of time is always costly."

The old man named a price. Carter managed not to gag.

"I'm putting your niece through the Sorbonne!"

Dufasse's hands splayed in a shrug. "You want quality and speed?"

"Of course I do," Carter said, and then sighed with resignation. "Done. Can you deliver them to the pier on time?"

"Look for the child."

"Also, I would appreciate it if you would send this wire. I'd rather not be seen doing it myself."

"As you wish. How about Portimão for the home port, and *Safe Bet* for a name?"

Carter chuckled. "I think he'd like that."

From Dufasse's shop, Carter had driven back to the Port Lympia area and found a boat outfitter. He ordered a new stern board identification for the *Safe Bet*, Portimão, and got assurance that he could pick it up in an hour.

Then he killed time over a good meal in an out-of-the-way café. Dufasse's niece was right on time, and with the new stern board in the trunk, Carter drove aboard the ferry for Bastia, Corsica.

It was dusk when he landed and drove south to Bonifacio, where he caught the last ferry to Sardinia. Now he was passing through Oristano, the halfway point south to Cagliari.

It was raining hard now, the huge drops slanting his way. The narrow, twisting road was dangerous even on a clear night, but Carter took chances to save time. It wouldn't do to arrive too long after midnight.

An hour later, he cut east and started down out of the hills toward the city. On the outskirts he stopped for gas and made the phone call.

Noreen answered on the first ring, and Carter sighed with relief. "You got the wire."

"Yes, I thought you were flying in."

"A little unforeseen problem. Is the big bird in?"

"Yes. He registered with a British passport under the name of Stern. I contacted him this afternoon."

"And his hardware?"

"In, stored at a mini-warehouse by East Pier Nine."

"Is that where the *Long Shot* is berthed?"

"Yes," Noreen replied. "There's a police guard on it. It's been impounded."

"I figured that. Was Trig able to locate Rollo's first mate, Carpenter?"

"Yes. He's waiting it out in a seaman's hotel, the Aurora. But when Trig mentioned your name, he said he would wait for you tonight in a waterfront bar, the Crow's Nest. It's near the pier."

"I'll find it," Carter said. "Have Trig keep checking the lobby and the hotel perimeters for unfriendlies."

"Will do. Nick . . ."

"Yeah?"

"I only got one room, and it's got a double bed . . ."

"Good for you. See you in a couple of hours. Keep it warm."

Well, I'll be damned, he thought, hanging up and returning to the car.

• • •

Carter passed the pier where the *Long Shot* was moored. When he was sure he had the whole scene in mind, he found a parking space and doubled back toward the rickety, swinging sign he had already spotted announcing the Crow's Nest to the world.

Inside was a long, low barroom typical of waterfront saloons around the world. The air was thick with smoke and the smell of stale beer and spilled liquor. This mingled with the stink of sweating, unwashed bodies.

There was an ancient jukebox blaring something the Godfather would love, and about two dozen customers at the bar shouting at each other over it to be heard. There were tables in the center filled with tired women, and booths along one wall partially filled with refugees from the tables who had managed to trade a feel for a beer.

It was an ordinary-looking port-town crowd, Carter thought to himself as he shouldered to the bar and ordered a beer. Nothing to distinguish its denizens from those in a dozen other joints he'd seen.

When he was sure of this, he searched and found Rowland's first mate, Nails Carpenter, in the extreme rear booth. Their eyes met, Carpenter nodded, and Carter oozed through the crowd to join him.

"Glad you remembered me."

"I never forget a face or a name," Carpenter growled.

He was on the hard side of fifty, about six feet spread over a stringy frame. His face was battered and pockmarked, and his eyes radiated nothing. They were weary eyes that had seen a lot of wars.

But he could sail anything that floated, and he was fiercely loyal to Rowland.

"What happened?" Carter asked.

The other man shrugged. "We put in here about a month ago, the man gets a good game goin' with the local politicos, and takes 'em good. They don't like it but they take it. Then Rollo meets this broad, about thirty, a real looker with hot pants.''

"And it turns out she's the mayor's wife."

"Yeah. The old man is pissed. He slaps an illegal gambling rap on Rollo, drops him in the tank, and throws away the key."

"When's the trial?"

Carpenter laughed. "Are you kiddin'? This is Sardinia. If there is a trial, it'll probably be about 1999. The mayor even owns our lawyer."

Carter nodded. The law in Sardinia was very flexible, usually bending toward the existing government. "How much do they want?"

"Fifty grand and the *Long Shot*."

"Too much," Carter hissed.

"That's what Rollo says."

"Okay," the Killmaster countered, "I just checked the boat. They only have one guard on it. Can you handle him?"

"Sure, but what good does it do?"

"Because I'm going to break him out tomorrow night. Now, here's what I want you to do . . ."

Carter shoved the clothing box under his left arm and knocked.

"Yes?"

"It's me."

The door opened a crack and he slid through. The only thing Noreen was wearing was lipstick, with a glass of scotch in her left hand.

"Your bath is drawn," she said with a grin.

"For one or two?"

"Two, of course."

He trailed clothes all the way to the bathroom and dropped gratefully into the hot water. She joined him, and for the next half hour pampered him with her hands and lips.

Finally he could take no more. "Bedroom," he rasped.

Dripping wet, they sprawled across the bed.

They were both ready, but Carter paused, letting his eyes devour her first. Everything about her body was beautiful. The brownish-pink buttons crowning her breasts were fully erect. Her waist was hourglass narrow, and her hips were full but solid.

Then she moved and Carter felt every full line of her pressed against him.

"You like that?" she purred.

"I like this." He kissed his way down the curve of her soft belly.

Her eyes closed and she started breathing through her teeth, hissing her breath in and out, arching her hips upward.

Carter felt her body shudder, relax, and then slither away from him.

"Your turn," she moaned, rolling him over and covering him with her body.

The next five minutes became controlled agony and ecstasy. Then Carter exploded with her and they both fell into a satiated tangle on the bed.

"You want another drink?" she asked after a while.

"No, sleep."

"What happens next?"

"We spring Rowland. You visit him tomorrow in jail and set it up."

"Me? How the hell am I going to get in there?"

"That clothing box I dropped at the door . . . get it."

She was back in seconds.

"Open it," he said, already feeling himself slipping away.

"What the hell is this?"

"Your uniform, Sister Noreen."

"*Me*? A *nun*? It'll never work! Nick . . ."

But he was sound asleep.

• • •

The officious guard barely inspected her passport and credentials before handing her over to a sleepy-eyed warden.

"This way, Sister."

He opened a steel door and led her down a row of shadowy cells. Though it was high noon outside, very little light penetrated the windowless stone walls of the jail.

The guard didn't bother with the cell-block light. It was dim, with only a single bulb at the far end.

He unlocked the third cell from the end and motioned her inside. "Just call when you are through, Sister."

"Bless you."

He locked the cell and moved away. Noreen waited until she heard the outer door clank shut before she turned.

The cell smelled sour. The walls were damp. Outside light from a narrow slit high in the wall threw a pale glow on an iron cot that swung chained against the wall.

A body was curled in a fetal position facing the wall under a ratty blanket.

She shook him by the shoulder. "Jim . . . Jim, wake up."

"Huh?"

"Wake up!" she hissed.

He rolled over and stared. Then he fumbled for a pair of glasses and put them on. "What the hell . . ."

"You are Jim Rowland?"

"Yeah. Who the hell are you?"

"I am your sister of mercy, come to save you."

Rowland blinked his one good eye and shook his head. "Look, lady, thanks but no thanks."

To his wide-eyed amazement the nun pulled her wide black skirts up to her waist.

"Jesus, what the hell . . ."

Around her waist was a rope ladder. She unwound it and dropped it into his lap. Then she sat beside him on the cot and folded her hands primly in her lap.

"Look, asshole," she said, smiling sweetly, "just shut up and listen."

Carter pushed himself away from the table with a sigh and lit a cigarette as he glanced from one to the other.

Ace Hardy sat, a cigar tightly clenched in one corner of his mouth, nervously eyeing the Russian.

General Mock looked tense and bone-tired. In fact, Carter thought, the general looked like a man about to crack.

Trig Muldune was carefully cleaning and oiling a snub-nosed Magnum .357. Of the three, he was the only one totally calm.

"Ace, we're set with this Harun Al-Bidi?"

"No sweat. We pay the price, he'll deliver."

"And the direction-finder?"

"Set up to intercept and ready to talk to us on the frequencies you gave me."

"Trig, the general's hardware is everything we'll need?"

"Everything," Muldune said. "Shit, we could start a small conventional war."

"It might turn into that," Carter chuckled, and turned to the general. "I think it's a foregone conclusion now. Your comrades have teamed up with the One Hundred Eyes to stop us."

Mock nodded wearily. "Yes, I am afraid so."

"You want to tell us the whole story?"

Mock sighed and massaged his temples with his fingertips. "It is Hajib Tutambe. When Macías fell in Guinea, he was able to get the government records out of the country. Moscow put pressure on and saved him from the firing squad."

"Who did they shoot instead?" Carter growled.

Mock shrugged. "Who knows, probably some poor beggar. In any event, there's no turning back for me now. I'll leave for Geneva this evening."

Carter nodded. "We'll send you the account numbers and keys as soon as we have them."

Hardy glowered first at Mock and then at Carter. "How do we know this Commie bastard won't just transfer the loot to one of his own accounts and then disappear?"

Trig Muldune answered, feeding shells into the .357. "One reason is, I'll hunt his butt down and blow him away."

"And the other reason," Carter added, "is that, if he does that, Arizona might just as well be on the moon. Right, General?"

"Don't worry, gentlemen, I am an honorable man. If I weren't, I wouldn't be betraying my country. If you'll excuse me?"

He rose and shuffled from the room. Noreen passed him coming in.

"God, how do they wear these things all the time? I'm soaking wet under it!" She glanced back toward the door where the general had just exited. "What's with him?"

"Believe it or not," Carter said, "I think it's guilt. How did you do?"

"No problem," she replied, splashing a little tonic over a lot of gin. "I gave him the money and the rope ladder. He says any one of the three night guards can be bribed to let him into the exercise yard after dark. We supply the diversion, he goes over the wall."

"Good," Carter said, nodding. "Trig?"

"The van's ready."

"Okay," the Killmaster said, rising. "Let's all get some rest. We go at midnight."

FIFTEEN

The long black skirts made a distinctive rustling sound as Noreen walked outward on the pier. The *Long Shot* was not difficult to spot. Besides being the largest of the pleasure boats, it was the only one being guarded.

Nails Carpenter had timed it perfectly. The incoming policeman and the one being relieved were both standing by the gangway.

"Good evening, gentlemen."

"Sister."

"Good evening, Sister."

Noreen handed her passport to one of the men. "I visited my unfortunate brother this afternoon, and he asked me if I might bring him a few things from the boat."

Both policemen exchanged uncomfortable glances. "I'm sorry, Sister, we have no authority . . ."

"It's his Bible. He's very lonely without it," Noreen urged.

"We have no keys to the lower decks, Sister. The magistrate . . ."

Noreen lifted her hand to reveal a ring of keys. "I have duplicates. Please, my son, it is such a small thing.

And surely you don't think that I . . ."

The two men did a Gary Cooper-type toe-in-the-sand routine, avoiding her eyes.

"I'll tell you what," she continued. "You can have a glass of wine while I get the Bible."

Without waiting for an answer, she moved up the gangway and across the deck. The two policemen had no choice but to follow. After all, she was a nun. What did it matter if they broke the rules for a nun?

Noreen unlocked the door to the main salon and swept inside, with the two of them close behind. She went right to a revolving liquor cabinet, unlocked it, and chose an expensive champagne.

"I'm sure my brother won't mind," she said with a little smile, popping the cork.

As she sprinkled a fine white powder into the two champagne glasses and poured, she looked around.

No expense had been spared. The spacious cabin was paneled in dark mahogany, with wall-to-wall carpeting and two luxurious chandeliers. The furniture was soft leather, and all the glassware beside the bar was cut crystal.

She passed the glasses to them on a silver tray, then poured herself a small sherry. "I thank you, and my brother thanks you."

They drank, she sipped, and blocked the champagne bottle with her body as she doctored the remaining wine with the last of the powder.

"Enjoy, gentlemen. I'll only be a minute."

She stepped into the next cabin, a combination living-sleeping area, and closed the hatch behind her. As she moved across the cabin, she peeled away the voluminous dress and habit to reveal a dark sweater and slacks.

On through the galley she went, and emerged on the fantail. Silently, she crept to the stern rail and dropped to her belly with her head slightly over the side.

"Nails?"

Instantly a figure in a black wet suit appeared and grasped the stern line. "Everything all right?" he whispered.

"It will take about five minutes."

"Time enough," he said, hoisting himself to the deck and handing her a screwdriver. "Get that side!"

In just five minutes they had the stern board nameplate changed.

"Let's go check on our sleeping beauties."

They retraced Noreen's steps to the main salon. Both policemen were out cold, beatific smiles on their slack faces.

Carpenter chuckled. "What was that stuff?"

"I don't know, but Nick said they would be in dreamland for about twelve hours."

"Good enough. Let's get 'em on deck."

Together, they got the two men on deck and to the stern. Without another word between them, they inflated a rubber raft and slipped it over the side. Carpenter tethered it to the stern rail with a line and climbed down. With Noreen's help, he got the policemen into the raft and then climbed back aboard.

"Get the bowline," he said, casting off the stern line and moving forward to the bridge.

Noreen ran forward and jumped to the dock. The cruiser engines purred to life, and as she jumped back on board, she felt their powerful thrust move the newly christened *Safe Bet* toward the outer bay.

Once again she moved to the stern, and watched the rubber raft bob behind them in the yacht's wake. Now and then she glanced at Nails Carpenter's figure on the bridge.

At the mouth of the bay, he turned to her and ran a finger across his throat. She fumbled with the knots until they came free, and then cast off the line.

In seconds, the little raft with its blissfully snoring cargo disappeared in the darkness.

God, she thought, *are they going to have a surprise in the morning!*

The jail was a horseshoe of buildings surrounded by a high wall with coils of barbed wire on top of it. The open end of the horseshoe was an exercise yard that opened into a small, inner courtyard.

Once the guards were bribed it would be Rowland's job to get over the inner wall with the rope ladder and into the outer courtyard.

Other than the chirp of crickets and the distant slapping of surf, there was no sound about the place as Carter dropped from the rear of the van.

"Twenty minutes," Muldune said from the dark interior.

"Sharp," Carter replied, and darted into the shadows under the wall.

Behind him, he heard the van door close and the vehicle move away. Walking at a measured pace, he moved around half of the four-square-block complex until he was at the front. Luckily, he met no pedestrians who would wonder why a man would be wearing a huge, hot greatcoat on such a humid night.

At a corner of the building he took a long swallow from a bottle of cheap wine, spit it out, and liberally doused his shoulders with the rest of it.

Just before entering the building, he took a large portable radio from beneath his coat and set it on a ledge beside the door.

Inside, he staggered to the night officer who sat behind a raised desk. "I want you to arrest my wife," he slurred in Italian.

"What?"

"My wife. I want you to arrest her. I come home, find her with the baker. They kick me out of the house. My house! Can you believe that?"

The officer sniffed the alcohol-blurred air and shook his head. "Name?"

"Bellini, Adolfo Bellini. She was naked, the bitch!"

"Sit over there. Here, fill out this complaint form."

Carter took the paper and pencil and crossed to one of the several small desks. As soon as the officer turned away, he took a strip of gunpowder squibs from beneath his coat, stripped the thin paper from the gummed side, and stuck it to one leg of the desk. A minute later he staggered to the soft drink machine. As he poked his money into the slot with one hand, he attached two more strips of squibs to the side of the machine.

"Men's?"

The duty officer waved him down a hall with barely a glance. "The right."

"*Grazie.*"

Carter planted two strips in the hallway and three more in the men's room. Staggering past the duty officer's desk on his return, he plastered the front of it with three more.

Fifteen minutes after he had entered, Carter teetered back up to the desk. He dropped the completed form in front of the officer, who didn't even look up.

"Goin' to get a drink, but I'll be right back."

"You do that."

"Wanna be there when you arrest that bitch."

Outside, he layered both sides of the door with squibs, and activated the alarm on the radio that would turn on the tape at the precise time. He then turned the volume up to full and walked across the street. In a darkened doorway he hunkered down, pulled a tiny transmitter from his pocket, and checked his watch.

Four minutes.

"I don't know, signore . . ."

"Ah, c'mon, Luigi!"

"My name is Antonio."

"Yeah, sure. Listen," Rowland implored, "just five minutes in the inner courtyard. I'm tellin' ya, I need some air. It's stiflin' in here. I feel like I'm gonna puke." He gagged for emphasis, and if that weren't enough, peeled off five more large lira notes. "Here, get your old lady some fancy underwear."

"Very well, signore, come along. But five minutes only!"

"Yeah."

Rowland slipped into his jacket to mask the roll around his middle made by the rope ladder.

The guard eyed him. "If you are hot, signore, why do you wear a jacket?"

Rowland shrugged. "I might get a chill outside. C'mon, let's go."

Three blocks away, the giant Olaf sat in the driver's seat of the van, paying no attention to the racket going on above his head.

On the van's roof, Trig Muldune and Ace Hardy tied the last leather thong that attached a sixteen-foot aluminum ladder to the luggage rails.

The ladder itself stood straight up in the air, and running down it from the top end was a second rope ladder. At the last minute, by the wall, Hardy would drop the ladder over the top of the wall, mashing down the barbed wire. At the same time, Muldune would throw the rope ladder so it would drop into the courtyard.

"How much time?" Hardy asked.

"Twenty seconds."

Hardy stomped the metal roof of the van twice, and the engine came to life.

Carter chanted, "Five . . . four . . . three . . . two . . . one . . ."

And suddenly the quiet of the night was pierced with

his own voice, magnified a hundred times by the radio's speakers across the street.

"This is the Reforma Army of Liberation!" his voice screamed. "You have ten seconds to release all the prisoners! If you do not conform to our demands . . ."

The duty officer stepped through the door with his hand on his holstered gun and looked, bewildered, up and down the street. He was just turning to the radio when World War III went off on both sides of the door.

He dived back into the building just as the timer in Carter's hand exploded the second set of squibs he had placed on the leg of the desk.

Not knowing or caring who was in the street, but positive he was under siege, the duty officer emptied his Beretta through the glass doors.

Leaving his coat and the transmitter in the doorway, Carter sprinted around the corner and headed toward the van that was already moving with the passenger door open.

He ran a few steps with it and dived in, slamming the door. Inside, he twisted his body and leaned out the window until he could see the two men on the roof.

"Set?"

"Set!" Muldune shouted back. "Give it hell!"

The van surged forward and Carter primed two flare pistols.

"Mama mia!" the guard gasped, clawing the carbine from his shoulder as he turned toward the explosions.

Rowland rabbit-punched him behind the left ear, and gave him a second one on the way down. The unconscious man had barely hit the ground before Rowland had retrieved all his lire and more from his pockets.

"So much for you and the horse you rode in on, bastard," Rowland murmured, sprinting for the inner wall.

As he ran, he uncoiled the rope ladder from his middle and found the end with the rapelling hooks by feel.

It took two throws before the hooks caught. When they did, he scrambled over the wall in seconds, and dropped to the other side. Halfway across the courtyard, flares illuminated the sky above the compound. Behind him, at the front of the building, all hell was breaking loose.

The rope ladder came down, hitting him across the face. He grabbed it, steadied it, and scrambled up. Just as he jackknifed onto the aluminum ladder he heard a voice shout, "He's up! Go!"

Rowland teetered halfway across the ladder as it was raised from the barbed wire and the van lurched forward.

Suddenly he was nose to nose with another face. "Ace!"

"Yeah, you son of a bitch, you owe me ten thousand bucks!"

"Jesus, Ace, this in no time—"

"Ten thousand bucks."

Rowland grinned sheepishly. "Ten it is, you crazy bastard. Now let me down!"

Hardy dropped to the roof and Rowland joined him.

"Nice to see you again, ol' buddy," Hardy said, clapping the other man on the back.

"Screw you," Rowland replied, hanging on for dear life as the van careened around a corner.

Twenty minutes later, they left the main highway and went down a dirt road to a deserted cove. A hundred yards out the *Long Shot/Safe Bet* circled, waiting to pick them up. The yacht's launch was bobbing in the surf, its engine idling.

As one, they piled into the launch. Noreen Parris, in a tiny string bikini, was at the helm. The instant they were all aboard, the engine roared, the bow lifted, and they shot toward the waiting yacht.

"Hello again, Jim," she shouted over the roar. "I'm

Noreen Parris, your sister of mercy."

Rowland hooted. "Hi, Noreen Parris. You got a nice ass."

"Oh, God," she groaned, "I can see I'm going to love a whole week with you."

"He grows on you," Carter chuckled, taking the wheel. "Remember, everybody in casual clothes or bathing trunks the minute we get aboard. We're millionaire yachtsmen just partying it up."

"That should be easy," Hardy said, lighting a cigar and passing a fistful out to the others.

"No sweat," Rowland smiled. "Where's the booze?"

SIXTEEN

Avenue d'Mer ran straight down to the commercial harbor at Berbera. The yacht and private pleasure craft harbor was about a mile away. That was where they tied up and continued their revels.

In between, showing themselves on deck in pairs or threes drinking champagne, Carter briefed them down below.

Early on the evening of *go*, Noreen and Muldune made a last recon. Ostensibly, they left the boat for supplies, but four times they walked past the Avenue d'Mer, snapping pictures with concealed cameras.

Developed, the film pretty well matched up with the field reports from General Mock.

The building contained working and sleeping quarters for twelve men. It was five stories high, with the first floor taken up with a fish market for cover. The second and third floors were living areas, and the fourth and top floors were the communications center.

They would go in, or over, from the building in the rear. It was a trucking terminal and warehouse, hardly used. There was only one old man on duty as a night watchman. He would be taken out with a hypodermic.

At midnight, they blacked out the boat and climbed into wet suits. Each man carried a silenced 9mm pistol with raised laser sight, an AK-47 modified for silencer, and a utility belt with a commando knife and extra magazines. Muldune and Olaf also looped rapelling lines with hooks around their shoulders.

Only five would go as an assault team. Noreen and Nails Carpenter would stay with the boat and be ready in case of a failure and retreat.

Just before the assault team slipped into the water, Carter gave them a last warning. "Remember, these people are brainwashed to their cause. They are geared up to die."

Muldune chuckled. "We'll just help them along, then."

One by one they slipped into the dark, murky water and swam the mile or so to the main harbor. They surfaced under a rotting pier, their objective directly across the street about a hundred yards away.

From here on in it would be very little talk and a lot of sign language. Carter made hand motions and they moved out by twos.

As soon as Hardy and Olaf disappeared into the shadows beside the building, Rowland and Muldune took off. When he could no longer see them, Carter himself slid across the street, just another shadow in the dimness.

The whole street was lined with warehouses, all of them five stories. All had huge doors and loading platforms. Carter joined the others at the small door in the larger one that opened to admit trucks.

Rowland was already doing a number on the lock.

"Spot the watchman?" Carter asked.

"Yeah," Trig Muldune replied. "He's sleeping like a baby in that room there with the lantern. We can probably just go around him."

"No," Carter said. "We can't chance it. Rollo?"

"It's open."

"Trig, go get him," Carter said.

The five of them slipped inside. Like a cat, Muldune faded away. He was back in two minutes.

"He won't wake up until noon," he said with a grin.

"Let's go," Carter growled.

In single file, they climbed an ancient set of wooden stairs and then a wooden ladder. A trapdoor let them out onto the roof only a few feet from the edge.

It was a good thirty feet across. All the windows in the other buildings sported blackout curtains, and its roof was as dark as a well.

Without being told, Muldune and the giant, Olaf, uncoiled the rapelling lines from their shoulders. Both hooks were made with hard rubber. To further deaden the sound, the spars themselves had been wrapped with foam from pillows aboard the *Long Shot*.

In the dimness they could make out two air-conditioning units, television antennas, and a raised area that probably masked a door to the lower floors.

"Stay away from the antennas," Carter whispered. "Ten to one they are for the transmitters and receivers."

Both men nodded and stood against the night sky. There was a whooshing sound as the hooks revolved around and around their heads and then sailed through the air.

One clamped to the raised edge of the roof; the other lit just beyond one of the air conditioners. Gently, Muldune pulled back on the line until a spoke dropped into the grate and held.

Both men tied off.

"Set," Muldune said.

"Let's go!" Carter hissed, rolling over the roof edge and hand-walking to the other side. The other four quickly followed, and the Killmaster nodded to himself with satisfaction when they took up positions on either side of the door.

Once again, Rowland used his magic fingers on the lock, and Carter was moving down a flight of stairs with the others tight behind him. All of them wore black canvas boat shoes so there wasn't a ripple of a sound.

Through a crack in the lower door, Carter perused the hallway. It was narrow and short with a door at either end. Above each door was an old-fashioned glass transom.

Carter patted Muldune on the shoulder and they moved out. Muldune dropped to his hands and knees, and Carter stood on his back. Through the door he could hear voices and the steady hum of electronic equipment.

Cautiously, he peered over the transom, made eye contact, and dropped back to the floor. At the other door Hardy and Olaf had done the same thing.

Hardy held up three fingers; Carter spread wide all five.

Rowland gently clicked off the safety on his AK-47, and took up a position on the stairwell in case they were surprised by a shift change.

When Carter saw that all four men were in place, their arms ready, he gave the start.

"Go!" he whispered.

Muldune's hand was already on the knob. Carefully he turned it, nodded at Carter, and then threw it wide.

The Killmaster rolled into the room and came up on one knee, firing. He took out all three men sitting at the consoles with one burst. Standing in the doorway behind him, firing over his head, Muldune took out the other two to their right.

Other than the soft thud of bodies hitting the floor and one coffee cup breaking, there was no sound.

The two men worked as a team, checking each body

to make sure of the kill. Thirty seconds after opening the door, they were back in the hall. Hardy and Olaf were already there.

There were no words, just nods, and they were headed down the stairs in single file.

The fourth floor was made up of arms storage, computers, and crates of propaganda leaflets.

There was a solo man sitting in a swivel chair with his feet on a desk. He was reading a magazine. When he sensed movement behind him, he looked up.

A single slug from Carter's 9mm pistol took off the side of his head.

"Nine down, three to go," Carter growled.

The third floor was a recreation room and kitchen. It was empty.

Two men slept soundly on cots in one of the cubicles on the second floor.

Olaf and Muldune dispatched them with knives.

"We're short one," Muldune hissed.

"Probably out getting boozed up or laid, or both," Hardy chortled.

"First floor . . . cellar," Carter said softly, and down they went.

The first-floor shop was empty, as was the cellar.

"Rollo, get back up top and switch one of the transmitters to our operating frequency. Radio Nails we're secure, and bring up Mock in Geneva. Tell him number one is down."

"Gotcha."

"And start familiarizing yourself with their code books and the equipment.

"Also, they are probably on a send-receive schedule. Memorize it. And go over the printouts of their old copy, so you can duplicate their language mannerisms on the key."

Rowland took off up the stairs.

"What about the twelfth guy?" Hardy asked.

"You're probably right," Carter replied. "He's on the town. We'll hear him when he starts up the front stairs. Meanwhile, it's burial detail time."

"Cellar?" Muldune asked.

"Yeah. Let's move."

Shallow graves were dug first, and then the bodies were wrapped in plastic bags and brought down. The covering up had just begun when they heard Number Twelve's key in the front door.

Like a shadow, Carter raced up the stairs and through the fish store on the first floor. On the second-floor landing, he braced his back to the wall opposite the door.

Less than a minute later, Number Twelve reeled through the door. Hardy had been right. His eyes were two bloodshot balls and his step was unsteady. Carter could smell the cheap booze on his breath from where he stood.

It took the man a full ten seconds to realize Carter wasn't one of the boys. When he did, the Killmaster spoke.

"You've got two choices . . . cooperate, or die."

Number Twelve jerked his coat aside with his left hand and went for a revolver in his belt with his right.

Carter put a five-shot burst from his automatic rifle in the middle of his chest. The body teetered for a second, and then bumped and thudded down the stairs.

Muldune's head appeared arond the corner. He looked at the corpse and then up at Carter.

"Clean sweep, O High Chieftain."

"Smooth as glass," Carter grunted. "Give him last rites. I'll be with Rollo."

"Right."

Carter hotfooted it up the stairs to the main communications room on the fifth floor. Rowland was just shutting down.

"Nails is cool. He's cranked up and ready to go."

"Good. Mock?"

"He says congratulations. The plane awaits in Djibouti. Pilot's name is Gildorf."

"Good enough. You think you can handle it?"

"Snap," Rowland said. "The schedule is mostly receive, and it's only once a day."

"Then it's all yours," Carter said. "Nails should be back by morning."

"No sweat."

Carter joined the others on the roof and they retraced their way back, taking the rapelling lines with them.

They had gone in at midnight. It was now just short of two in the morning.

SEVENTEEN

The pilot, Gildorf, was like a man without eyes or ears. He flew people or things anywhere in the world, for a price.

Carter smiled inwardly. Mock had good contacts.

The whole team slept during most of the flight across the continent. It was a seven-hour flight. With the time change, they reached the Atlantic Ocean at two in the afternoon. A half hour later they crossed over the island of São Tomé, and soon after that spotted the *Sea Breeze* idling in a large circle back and forth across the equator.

Luckily, the sea was like glass, enabling Gildorf to set the plane down as if it were on terra firma.

Carter rechecked the itinerary with the pilot. He would fly north and land in Lagos, Nigeria's capital. Once there, he would hibernate, checking his radio every four hours, night and day. When the message *It's time to follow the Saharan sun* came over, he would take off and pick them up again in the same spot.

Satisfied, Carter and the others piled into the launch.

An elaborate meal awaited them aboard Hardy's yacht. After they had eaten, Carter dragged out Mock's report on the One Hundred Eyes station at Bata.

The briefing took a full three hours. By the end of it, the *Sea Breeze* was pulling into a slip at the Bata marina.

They all went on deck. Three miles up the coastline, perched on a bluff overloking the ocean, sat the old colonial villa that was their target.

"That's it," Carter said. "The play's about the same. We go at midnight."

Without a word, Hardy, Muldune, and Olaf went below to recheck the hardware.

Carter glanced up at the moon, an artificial-looking golden ball that was sending a bright shimmering light over several miles of sea behind them and three hundred feet of sheer cliff face in front of them.

At the top, on the very edge of the cliff, was the villa. It was an enourmous, rambling, three-story structure belonging to a long-gone colonial era. At the side, coming down the cliff face, a set of narrow steps was cut into the stone.

"It'll be tricky in the moonlight," Hardy said, killing the engine of the launch.

Carter nodded. "That's why I'll go first . . . take the sentries out." According to Mock's intelligence, there were always two, one walking the stone path and one at the top guarding the tall iron gates.

They were drifting now at the headland marking the approach to the cove. Carter felt the launch roll as Olaf dropped anchor. He looked over at Noreen. She was nervous but she managed a smile.

The AK-47 looked awkward in her hands, but he knew that Hardy had taught her how to use it that afternoon. She would stay in the launch and hit anyone if he managed to elude the team and try for an ocean escape.

"Watch for my signal," Carter said, and rolled over the side of the launch.

He swam effortlessly around the breakwater and struck off across the cove. When he reached the pier, he sidestroked from timber to timber until he felt his flippers hit rocks. Quietly, he pulled himself up clear of the water and shucked the flippers. From the oilskin bag on his back he took his pistol, the Kalashnikov, and the canvas sneakers. When the sneakers were on and tied, he started up the path, staying as low as possible.

The stone path curved like a snake up the cliff face. Halfway up, he heard the soft pad of feet coming down.

Carter accelerated to the curve and dropped flat, holding the pistol in both hands in front of him. His belly did a soft flip-flop when the footsteps stopped.

Then he saw the flare of a match around the curve, heard a fast intake of breath, then a long exhale.

Seconds later the man walked around the curve, the burning glow of his cigarette helping Carter's aim.

The Killmaster pressed the trigger, centered the laser beam a foot below the cigarette's glow, and put two slugs in the man's chest.

The *phhht* sound was still in his ears as he caught the body and eased it silently to the ground. Without a second's pause, he stepped over it and continued his ascent.

Near the top he paused. The villa was dark except for a few lights on the first floor. A scrolled lantern hung just inside the closed iron gates. From the gates to the rear of the house was about fifty yards of garden.

Somewhere in there was the second guard. And then Carter saw him, lounging against a tree just twenty feet inside the gate. He, too, was smoking and gazing up at the sky.

The Killmaster crept forward and balanced the pistol on one of the iron cross-grates. The laser beamed on and he fired once. It was enough, but, just in case, he put two more slugs into the body as it slid down the tree.

Taking a penlight from his bag, he pointed it down the cliff and flashed it three times. Then he went to work on the padlock. Just as it opened, he heard a sound behind him. Running feet . . . bare feet.

Out of the corner of his eye he saw a huge black dressed only in a swimsuit.

It hit him at once. One of them had gone for a midnight swim, and somehow Carter had gotten by him in the water without being seen.

One of the man's powerful arms swung in an arc. Carter saw the glint of moonlight on a long blade, and rolled. At the same time, he kicked out, catching the man in the crotch, deflecting the knife that now swished past his head. A heavy body crashed down on top of him and the man jerked the knife clear as Carter grabbed the thick wrist.

They rolled over and over, locked in a hideous embrace, Carter holding the knife hand, his legs in a death-grip scissors around the black's muscular belly. A free hand went to Carter's throat, a thumb mashing the windpipe closed. They thrashed about on the ground. Carter felt his throat closing, his breathing becoming painful. He yanked at the wrist with his hand, and momentarily the choking eased up. Carter gave a mighty surge, rolling and shoving with his right hand, forcing the knife into the other's chest.

The black grunted and strained. The knife came out of his chest and he struggled to turn it around toward Carter. Carter twisted again, exerting every ounce of his strength, pushing, pressing, squeezing, then giving a desperate lunge that sank the knife to its hilt a second time in the deep chest. The man screamed once, a scream that turned to a burbling gurgle, and blood spurted up in Carter's face.

Carter staggered to his feet, shaking his head, just as the others hit the top of the path.

"You okay?" Hardy exclaimed.

"Yeah," Carter panted. "He surprised the shit out of me."

"We saw him come out of the water about two minutes behind you, but there was nothing we could do until you signaled."

To the side, Trig Muldune was playing a shielded flash across the black's face. "Nick, lad, you are awfully good, or awfully lucky. Or both."

Carter joined him. "What do you mean?"

"You just took out the baddest of the baddest. That's Jacob Borassa."

Carter looked down at the dead man. He looked meaner dead than he had alive. The Killmaster shivered, unslung the AK, and led the way through the gate. "C'mon!" he hissed.

Hardy and Muldune each took a side entrance over verandas and through French doors. Olaf went around to the front, and Carter took the rear. He was surprised when he found the door unlocked.

It opened onto a great room. Carter moved through it and then through two more rooms into an empty hall, where he ran into Muldune.

"Anything?"

"*Nada*," said the ex-SAS man. "My guess is they're all in the communications room or up in the bedrooms."

Carter nodded and sprinted across the hall. He unlocked the front door, and Olaf slipped inside.

"Upstairs," Carter said, "take each room one at a time. Ace and I've got 'em boxed down here."

The two men disappeared up a wide, grand staircase, and Carter moved toward a pair of mammoth wooden doors. Light seeped from beneath the doors.

He attached a lanyard to the pistol and draped it over his neck after jamming a new clip home. Then he readied the AK and crouched down in front of the doors to wait.

Five, then ten minutes passed. At fifteen minutes

there was a growling scream from the upper part of the villa, quickly followed by the chatter of machine gun fire.

Carter lunged forward, firing at the door's locks. He hit the crack between the two doors like an offensive tackle, and burst into the room.

There were five, two at the consoles, one at a portable bar pouring coffee and two at desks to his right and left.

The gun shook in his hands, and the coffee pourer reared back and crashed into the wall. Carter fell, arcing the still-spurting rifle toward the man at the desk to his right. The slugs stitched red across the man's chest and he disappeared behind the desk.

Carter was diving to join him, when the room suddenly exploded with the sound of high-caliber fire. He felt the hiss of slugs past his head, and hot flowers blossomed a foot above him on the wall.

At the same time, the French doors crashed inward and Hardy came through them like a bull. The two at the consoles were on their feet now, and armed.

But their attention had been on Carter. Suddenly they were confused.

That confusion killed them as Hardy took them out with one burst.

That left one, the man at the other desk. To Carter's surprise, he dropped his gun and walked toward the center of the room with his hands in the air.

"You speak English?" Carter barked, following the movement with the AK-47.

He shook his head.

"French? Spanish?"

Suddenly the man bolted toward the wall and what looked like a breaker box. He clawed the door open and was reaching for the master switch when Hardy cut him down.

"What was that for?" Carter asked.

"The joint's wired," Hardy grunted. "I saw the

charges outside under the eaves. That's probably the master switch to make the whole place go boom-boom."

"Nice people," Carter growled as Olaf and Muldune drifted into the room.

"Sorry about that," Muldune said. "The bloody bastard was awake with his gun in bed."

"It worked out. How many upstairs?"

"Three," Muldune replied.

Carter fumbled a walkie from his belt. "Noreen?"

"Here."

"We're secure. Head back to the *Sea Breeze*. I'll radio you when it's a go."

"Will do."

Then the Killmaster turned to the others.

"Okay, Ace, let's go to work."

The net was set up by Hardy with his people. They established a direction-finding triangle, with Rowland in Somalia on one corner, Carter in Equatorial Guinea on the other, and Hardy's people in Mauritania on the third.

The next morning's transmissions from the One Hundred Eyes' home base lasted a full half hour. It was more than long enough. Only fifteen minutes after their transmitters shut down, Mauritania came up on the alternate frequency with the grid coordinates.

"Can you figure it out?" Carter asked.

Ace Hardy nodded, already poring over an enlarged grid map of Niger. Twenty minutes later he looked up.

"Got it. I can put Harun Al-Bidi's caravan within two hundred yards of it."

"Half done," Carter sighed, and went to another of the transmitters to bring up Rowland by voice.

"*Safe Bet*, this is *Sea Breeze*, do you read? Come in. Over."

"Got you, *Sea Breeze*. Over."

"We are secure. Do you have anything on step two? Over."

"Does a bear shit in the woods?" came the cackling reply. "All kinds of it, my man . . . account numbers and all. The Red Man in Alpsville has it, and will reply when he's sure he and his people can pick up. To you."

"Anything on amounts?" Carter replied. "Over."

"Fat city. Tell the Ace that I'll even pay him his interest on the ten grand. Hell, tell him we can buy a small country somewhere and retire! Over."

"Stay in touch. Out."

"Will do. Out."

While they waited, Hardy put a timer on the master switch as per Carter's orders. It was set for thirty minutes after the switch was pulled.

At noon, Rowland's familiar low voice came back on the radio. General Mock had all he needed to start shifting the One Hundred Eyes' funds into accounts he now controlled.

"Call Gildorf in Lagos. Have him meet us right after dark."

At dusk, the little party headed back down the cliff path toward the waiting launch from the *Sea Breeze.*

Just before Carter left, he brought Rowland up again.

"Charges set?" he asked.

"Oh, yeah."

"Vacate *now.*"

"Righto, my man. See you in Geneva!" The radio went dead.

The last thing Carter did before leaving the room was pull the master switch.

EIGHTEEN

Harun Al-Bidi was a white-haired old man who ruled his people with an iron hand, as had his father and grandfather before him. They were nomads, and they obeyed only the laws of their tribe and Allah.

They were also fierce warriors who didn't mind taking the infidels' money to kill other infidels.

Gildorf deposited them at the foot of the Aïr Mountains, and found a café in a nearby village to wait. Reluctantly, Noreen Parris stayed with him. From there it was a four-hour trip by Land-Rover to rendezvous with the caravan.

The old man had already sent out scouting parties at Hardy's request. They had come up with gold.

"No wonder it couldn't be found," Carer sighed, gazing down from a dizzying height into a deep gorge almost completely hidden by overhanging ledges of rock.

"And if it was," Hardy added, "it looks like any sleepy oasis village."

Because that was just what it was, a village of stucco and wooden huts stretching for a few hundred yards in the gorge. But at the end of the village, completely disguised from the air, was the mouth of a gigantic cave. It was from this cave that Hajib Tutambe was mounting his plan to take over Africa.

Carter guessed that all the living quarters, the arms, and the communications center would be in the cave.

Raising a powerful pair of field glasses to his eyes, he spotted the one tip-off that the village wasn't all that it seemed.

Everywhere he looked, there were only men and a few women. No children and no animals.

The old chief appeared at Carter's side. "My men are ready. We will go into the village just before dawn, when sleep claims its tightest grip on their minds."

And, Carter thought, *we* will go in an hour before that.

It was two hours before dawn, the darkest part of the desert night. Deep in the wadi there were a few small fires, but they were banked high, giving off little or no light.

Carter and Muldune had already come across two sentries. Both had been bored and on the verge of sleep themselves. They had posed no problem and had given no alarm before they died.

Besides the silenced 9mm pistols and knives, both men wore heavy utility belts around their waists and packs on their backs. The belts were loaded with timer detonators, flash and smoke grenades, and extra magazines. The backpacks held cubes of plastique. Also, they both wore infrared night-vision goggles.

Slowly they made their way along the middle line of the ridge, their destination the flat plateau of rock leading backward from the mouth of the cave and serving as its roof.

Carter felt Muldune's hand on his belt and stopped at once. The other man pointed down. The Killmaster looked.

Six inches in front of him he saw the trip wire.

He nodded, gingerly stepped over it, and moved on
with Muldune close behind him. There were four more
of them before they found themselves on a rocky out-
cropping above the roof of the cave.

Side by side, they crawled down as far as they could
go, and then dropped silently the last few remaining
feet. There they paused, listening intently, forcing their
ears to separate the few sounds around them until they
heard what they were after: fans pumping fresh air into
the cave through drilled vents. A few minutes later they
found the first one.

Carter gently raised the housing without touching the
fan, while Muldune rigged a line drop on three cubes of
plastique. He showed the detonator fuse to Carter, who
held up two fingers. Muldune set it, jammed its needle
edge into the plastique, and pushed it between the roof
line and the revolving fan.

Slowly he played out twenty-five feet, and mouthed
the word bottom.

Carter nodded, and Muldune played out enough line
across the roof to secure it as the Killmaster replaced the
vent cover.

In the next forty minutes they doctored sixteen more
vents and draped a healthy amount of the plastique over
the front edge of the cave. The timers were staggered so
it would become a constant series of chaotic explosions.
They hoped the plastique would serve two purposes
from the first blast on: total destruction and total confusion.

"Okay," Carter whispered, "let's find us some
clothes."

At the rear of the cave roof they found stairs cut into
the stone. Three quarters of the way down, another
ledge began and ran several hundred yards along the last
of the gorge, ending in the solid stone face of the cliff.

It was Muldune who spotted the fakery first. He patted Carter's shoulder and then motioned the Killmaster to run his hand along the stone. Carter did, and nodded.

The "stone" was actually papier-mâché built over a wooden frame, much the same as bogus mountains on a movie set.

The two men exchanged glances. They had already guessed that Hajib Tutambe would have an escape exit. Chances were they had found it.

At the bottom of the stairs, one half of that guess came true. There was a wide steel door set flush into the rock.

Five minutes later, moving back under the papier-mâché canopy, part two of the guess proved out. There, in an open section, sitting like a giant insect, was a Hughes 500-D chopper. Further investigation told them that a section of the canopy was retractable.

Neat, Carter thought, *very neat.*

Then they heard voices, two of them, near the bubble canopy at the front of the chopper.

Without being told, Muldune skittered away behind the machine like a night animal to come up on their flank.

The Killmaster made sure he gave Muldune more than enough time before stepping around the front of the chopper.

Both guards were so surprised that they could only stand and gawk, their rifles leaning harmlessly against the chopper's landing gear.

At last one of them realized what was happening, and dived for his gun. Carter surged forward just as Muldune dropped a garrote around the other one's neck and dragged him, gagging, to the ground.

Carter caught his man in the face with a dropkick and sent his commando knife through the man's throat before he could recover.

Soundlessly, they dragged the lifeless bodies back among a pile of fuel drums and stripped them of their

warming outer robes. Carter and Muldune dressed and
took up the two men's positions at the chopper.

Just to be on the safe side, Carter crawled up into the
machine and severed all the hydraulic lines.

"How long until the first boom?" he asked, dropping
silently back to the ground.

"Sixteen minutes," Muldune grunted. "Think we can
smoke?"

"Why not?" Carter chuckled. "They were."

The timers worked perfectly. One moment all was
serene, and the next all hell was breaking loose.

The top of the cave went up like Vesuvius, except that
there was no lava, only a lot of smoke, spurts of vivid
orange flames, and bits of stone flying everywhere.

Carter darted from under the canopy far enough to
see up the gorge. The sight was something he wouldn't
forget.

Harun Al-Bidi had sent forty or fifty men down in the
darkness. In the light from the explosions, Carter could
see them on both hillsides.

As the followers of the One Hundred Eyes ran from
the mouth of the cave, Al-Bidi's men on the hillsides cut
them down with continuous fire.

And then the finale began. Over the mouth of the
gorge, silhouetted against the gray dawn, came another
hundred men on horseback. They rode with their knees,
leaving both hands free to fire their rifles and machine
pistols.

Carter didn't know how, but he could actually hear
their blood-curdling screams of battle over the gunfire
and explosions. It made ripples run up his spine.

My God, he thought, *they wouldn't have to shoot you
to kill you. They could scare you to death first!*

He was sure now that he was seeing a tiny scene of the
Apocalypse. Even without the advantage of blowing up
most of the One Hundred Eyes in the cave, they

wouldn't have had a chance in the open again Harun Al-Bidi's hordes.

"Nick!"

He turned. Muldune was frantically waving him back to the chopper. Then he saw why. The massive steel door was opening.

There were five of them surrounding a sixth man. All of them were in Bedouin robes except the sixth man, the one in the center of the group. He was dressed in a Western-style business suit.

He was tall and thin, with graying hair and a gaunt face as black as night. Even at that distance Carter could see his dead, predator's eyes, and knew that this was Hajib Tutambe.

They were about thirty yards away when Muldune whispered, "No prisoners?"

"No prisoners!" Carter hissed, and opened up with his AK-47.

It was a withering fire, evoking screams from the surprised men.

But even as they died, Tutambe's loyalists closed ranks to protect their leader.

"Shit," Muldune suddenly cried, "I'm hit!"

"Bad?"

"Don't think so . . . thigh."

Using his own falling men as a shield, Tutambe turned and fled back toward the steel doors.

"Get the bastard, Nick!"

Carter took off, discarding the bulky automatic rifle and bringing the laser pistol into play.

Instead of going through the doors, Tutambe turned left and raced up the stone stairs to the cave's roof.

He's got a second alternative, Carter thought. *Somewhere he's got a Land-Rover, or maybe even another helicopter.*

Carter saw him race up the steps, pausing for only a second to fire once at his pursuer. Rock chips flew to

Carter's left, but he didn't even pause.

At the top of the roof, Carter saw that his prey had already gained the ridge and was climbing.

Again the man paused, and the crack of a revolver sounded, heavy, in the open air.

Carter carefully squeezed off three shots, aiming all around the flash of the gun: he heard the bullets clanging off the stone and whipping giddily in the air.

All three were misses, and Tutambe was again scrambling up the ridge.

Carter followed now at a safe distance, pulling two flash grenades from the belt at his waist.

When he was sure the other man had reached the top, he began to climb again himself. At the same time, he kept his ears attuned. There was no sound above him. Somewhere Tutambe was lurking, waiting.

Carter didn't hesitate. He sprinted to the very top of the ridge and went over in a roll. He didn't see Tutambe, but he heard the scrape of the man's shoes as he stood to fire.

Carter rolled both grenades in the direction of the sound, and kept his own body rolling as slugs hissed by his head, chipping stone all around him.

He kept his eyes shut tight until he heard the two grenades go off. Then he waited the requisite time, opened his eyes, and looked.

Tutambe stood between two rocks at the very edge of the cliff, screaming, his hands over his blinded eyes.

Carter took aim until the laser was dead center. Then he squeezed off a shot, and kept firing until the pistol clicked empty and Tutambe's body gracefully took flight off the cliff.

Carter came forward and picked up the briefcase the man had dropped. There was no need to check its contents. He already knew that Mock's passport to freedom —and very damning evidence against the general's former comrades concerning their propping up of the old Macías regime—was now in his hands.

He looked down across the gorge to the cave. There was only sporadic firing now, and very little cleanup left. Between the plastique and the munitions inside the cave, it was no more than rubble. It would be a tomb for the men of the One Hundred Eyes buried inside it.

Harun Al-Bidi's men would take care of the rest of the cleanup. The desert would swallow up all trace.

Sighing with relief and clutching the briefcase, Carter descended to the floor of the gorge, to find Hardy and Muldune and the Land-Rover.

Carter sat in the far rear of the plane, sipping a scotch and watching the giant, Olaf, put a fresh dressing on Muldune's wound. Beside him, her face like stone, was Noreen Parris.

"I'm sorry," he said.

She shrugged. "Nothing?"

"Nothing," Carter replied. "You can't print a word of it. It's got to be as if it never happened."

"What if Washington decides to use that?" she said, nodding to the briefcase at Carter's feet.

"If they do," the Killmaster sighed, "you know the public will never know about it."

She sighed in turn, and suddenly smiled. "Shit. It was a hell of a story."

"Yeah, it was," he chuckled. "Tell you what. Why don't you write it up as a novel—an international espionage thriller? Nobody would ever believe it could really happen."

Ace Hardy came back from the cockpit, interrupting them. "I got Geneva up, Nick."

Carter pulled himself from the bucket seat and moved forward. "General?" he said into the hand mike.

"Congratulations," came Mock's voice.

"Thank you," Carter replied. "How about there?"

"As you Americans say, our cup runneth over. Tell

your friends that they are all very rich capitalists."

Beside him, Carter saw Hardy lighting a cigar and rubbing his hands together.

"And you'll be glad to know, General, that we have the goods. I don't think your former comrades in Moscow will send a team for your skin."

"That, Nicholas," Mock replied, "is a relief."

Carter laughed out loud. "You're going to love Arizona, General."

DON'T MISS THE NEXT
NICK CARTER

EAST OF HELL

A string of taxis waited across the street to solicit fares. Carter spotted one with dark windows. In Portuguese, he asked the driver to wait for him.

The two men he'd seen on the superstructure of the ship were off first and in a hurry. They were both dressed in lightweight white suits. He couldn't see their faces, but he recognized their walk and the way they carried themselves. They were definitely the Russian agents.

The two were met by a man driving a black Mercedes 300SL. It took off quickly, heading south along Avenida do Dr. Oliveria Salazar.

"Where are we heading?" he asked his driver as they cruised along the wide boulevard fifty yards behind.

"Half a mile to the casino. Most tourists go there."

Carter sat back. These were not tourists. He'd just have to wait and see.

As they approached the casino, a round, twelve-story structure, the Mercedes pulled up and the Russians entered in a hurry.

Carter told his driver to wait. Inside the casino, the floor was divided into a number of small rooms, each luxuriously decorated with flocked wallpaper in reds and oranges, each room specializing in a different game: roulette, blackjack, chemin de fer, craps, or fan-tan.

The men he was following stopped to talk to a pit boss in a blackjack room. A pall of smoke drifted over the heads of the players. Carter looked over the setup. Not a chair was empty at the four tables. Players of every nationality bet with paper money that dealers accepted, folded carefully, and stacked in long wooden trays. Cards were dealt slowly and deliberately. There was no way you could win at those tables, he thought. One prerequisite of a winning night at blackjack was a large volume of hands, and that would be impossible here.

The two men moved off to a back room with the pit boss. The man was a Westerner built like a block of granite with a face to match. The Russians would have fooled Carter if he hadn't known they were allies of Moltsovski. They didn't have any of the rough, heavy features normally associated with the KGB or GRU.

The door closed behind them.

Carter's Spectacles Chen disguise was holding up well enough. No one seemed to be paying him any attention. He moved quickly to the door, opened it, and slipped in.

The room was round and contained not one stick of furniture. It did contain four grinning street fighters dressed in red. Carter needed no further proof that the Russians worked with the Fang tong.

With that thought, he grabbed for the door handle, only to find that the inside of the door had none. He flipped Hugo from its chamois sheath as the Fang warriors started to circle. Each carried a war hatchet and a wicked-looking double-sided knife.

One lunged, and Carter ducked under the charge, slipping Hugo between unguarded ribs. Before the startled man fell, his heart beating its last, the Killmaster turned him around, reached for his heels, and spun him in a circle, knocking the remaining three to the floor.

Before they recovered their weapons, Carter was on two of them, holding one by the chin as he ripped Hugo across an unguarded neck. The other Carter soon had in a choke hold, his spine almost ready to crack.

The fourth man panicked. He ran for a concealed door, opened it, and headed into an adjoining room. Carter whipped the neck of the street fighter an inch further and, as the sound of breaking bone reverberated around the room, took off after the fleeing man. He got there before the door could close.

The next room was square, and housed unused gambling equipment. In the far corner, the two Russians stood with the pit boss, their heads together. As Carter entered, they pulled their guns and opened fire.

Wilhelmina slipped easily into his hand. From behind an overturned craps table, Carter waited. He could hear the excited Fang warrior scream at the Russians in Cantonese, and their terse, guttural replies.

The Killmaster left the safety of the table to get closer to the men. One Russian took another shot at him, but he was too slow. Wilhelmina answered, the noise bouncing off the walls. A 9mm slug tore off the side of the Russian head, splattering blood and brain matter into the air.

A door was opened at the far end of the room. The pit boss and the surviving Russian scrambled through before Carter could get a shot at them, but he did manage to put a slug through the last of the Fang street fighters as the frightened Chinese tried to slip through.

Carter knew that his only chance of finding Moltsovski was to get that second Russian and question him. He stopped a few seconds to search the dead agent; he found only empty pockets. The fashionable tropical suit had no labels.

The dead Fang warrior was sprawled across the doorway, his body wedged between the door and the frame. From the windows of the next room, Carter saw that he was now at the back of the casino. He raced for a door, flung it open, and ran around to the front of the building. He had lost his horn-rimmed glasses in the fight with Fang. The humid air brought out rivulets of sweat. Makeup was slowly dripping off his chin. Spectacles Chen was leaving the scene and Carter was emerging whether he liked it or not.

As he rounded the building, gun in hand, Carter noticed the black Mercedes racing off. Running toward his waiting cab, he slipped Wilhelmina back to her holster.

"Follow the black Mercedes!" he yelled at his driver who was leaning against the front fender talking to friends.

> —From EAST OF HELL
> Coming in July 1987

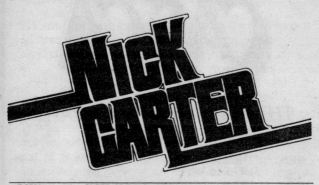

THE ETERNAL MERCENARY
By Barry Sadler